THE SHIFTING FAE: BOOK ONE

BY

ELIZA TILTON

THE MOONLIT WOODS

Cover art by Eliza Tilton

www.elizatilton.com

Give feedback on the book at:
elizatilton@gmail.com
Twitter: @elizatilton

First Edition

Printed in the U.S.A

“Ever has it been that love knows not its own depth until the hour of separation”

-Kahlil Gibran

Author's Note

If these characters seem a tad familiar, it's because this series was originally released under a pen name a few years ago. The stories were novellas and while I loved the world I'd created, it wasn't working. These characters needed more depth and for their tales to be told in the right way.

I made the decision to take down the series and it's been re-written and re-imagined into a full-length epic Fantasy Romance series with a fleshed-out world, plenty of action, and swoon worthy romance.

For those of you who have met our heroine and hero before, I hope that you love their new adventure and stay along for the ride.

Eliza

ONE

ROSALIE

Red marks covered my wrists where the chains had worn down my skin. The magical dampeners turned me from a wild storm into a useless kitty cat. Two weeks I had been locked in this wagon, traveling to the magical city of Farrow's Gate where I was to be offered to the city's magistrate, Lord Demious. A man whose high magic was as twisted as his black heart.

The barred window allowed me to view my temporary home. The slave trader who bought me only told me where I was going, not why. Traders could be devilish creatures with their bizarre wands and whips of freezing. If I hadn't been on the brink of starvation and weak, I may have slaughtered that pity of a troll where he stood.

But I had no choice, no say at all. In a desperate plea to save my family's home, I trusted the wrong person, and now . . .

Cerulean grass covered the estate grounds, swirling with vibrant hues of violet wildflowers. The stories surrounding Farrow's Gate always spoke of its ethereal beauty and how the wild magic in the land morphed the area into a kaleidoscope of colors.

All along the road leading to the white brick mansion, glimpses of iridescent butterflies and birds with gossamer wings flew in and around the magical wood. A large monarch, bigger than my fist, flew alongside the carriage, leaving a trail of glittering sparkles in its wake.

If I was going to be forced to live here, at least it was pretty.

When we arrived at the mansion, servants came to meet us. Two human girls rushed to the wagon, where they stood and waited. The driver unlocked the door and helped me out.

In the top corner window of the mansion, near a weeping willow with the prettiest lavender flowers, stood a man, watching. Being too far to see clearly, I could only make out his dark hair.

"Your new home," the driver said, and led me to the two girls. "This is Ara and Luna. They'll bring you to your quarters."

I wanted to be angry with the driver for leaving me here, but he was just a delivery man. I was the fool who trusted a troll wearing overalls and a top hat.

The servants smiled, though the taller one held a hand to her nose, my stench wafting on the afternoon breeze. Even I couldn't stand to be around myself, the odor of piss and other things clinging to my ragged dress.

Mouthing a sorry, I followed the two girls, who looked like twins with their matching blonde buns, mouselike features, and navy dresses, inside the regal home.

Question after question buzzed through my mind as we walked down the shimmering blackish golden marble corridors. Every wall decorated in lavish oil paintings and stuffed heads of wild creatures, ranging from an elk to the baby drakes that roamed far beyond the Crescent Mountains. My heart sank when I saw a massive black spiral horn. Even a wild thing like me knew how rare and mighty a night unicorn was—and this bastard had slaughtered it?

Wicked. Just like the stories.

The twins brought me to a less decorated wing on the east side of the house. I assumed these were the servants' quarters or something

less appealing. Honestly, I was happy just to be out of the wagon and on my feet. Two weeks of sitting in my own urine made any place more appealing than that horrid wagon. I could only imagine what I smelled like.

We entered a bedroom, bigger than I expected with a few floor length windows surrounded by cream drapes dotted with tiny rosebuds. The beige fluffy blanket on the four-post canopy bed added to the softness of the room. A table and two chairs sat adjacent to one of the windows. Fresh pink peonies had been placed in an ivory vase, igniting the room with floral magic.

"We'll run you a bath and come back to help you dress. You'll be brought to dinner where you'll meet Lord Demious," the taller twin said.

"Dinner? Do the servants normally eat with the master?"

They looked at each other, then at me. "No, my lady, but you are not a servant."

My heart thumped against my chest. If I wasn't bought as a slave, what were his intentions?

Before I could ask any more questions, the girls finished drawing the bath and left me alone. I peeled off the grime covered clothes I'd lived in for weeks and stepped into the warm water. For a moment, I forgot about everything else and let the water soak into my skin. I couldn't remember the last time I had bathed. Though

I was sure it was in a cold stream somewhere near the wilds of Haven.

While my home was only a two day's ride from Farrow's Gate, the troll had brought me further east before handing me off to the driver who brought me here. Based on the passing glimpses of the road, we hadn't traveled on the main merchant roads which made me wonder why. If Lord Demious had bought me for whatever reason, why wouldn't the driver take the shortest route?

Taking the soap, I rubbed my skin, revealing the pale ivory. Mother had always commented on my fair skin and crimson hair. A perfect doll. Even though Mother saw my beauty as a blessing, I didn't. I ran my fingers through my hair, trying to untangle the mop of knots, but failed miserably.

"Need some help, my lady?"

I turned my head and saw the shorter twin, standing by the bed with a bundle of clothes.

"Yes, please. I don't think I'll ever get these out," I said and pulled at my long hair.

She nodded and quietly sat on a stool behind me, leaving my dinner attire on the bed. "Relax and I'll take care of this. Luna is preparing your clothes for dinner."

I closed my eyes and leaned back while Ara pulled my hair and dumped a cool liquid on it.

Taking a comb, she ran it against my scalp and down, breaking the knots and doing it with a soft touch. It didn't take long for my hair to be completely combed and cleaned.

Luna entered the room just as I was stepping out of the tub and drying off. She smiled and handed me undergarments, which I slipped into. The dress she had brought swirled with the color of autumn. Beautiful sunset oranges and hazy reds trailed the skirt while the bodice was an auburn brown dotted with tiny golden crystals. I gasped when they tightened the corset and forced my chest to be more prominent, which was unnecessary considering how large my breasts were to begin with. In fact, the dress accentuated them so much I wondered if they were being served for dinner.

The girls worked on twirling and pinning my hair until little tendrils covered my neck. They ended my primping with a stunning jeweled black collar necklace with a glittering crystal in the center. Once they clasped the collar on my neck, they removed the magical dampeners on my wrists.

I searched for my inner flame but found darkness instead. Was it the collar?

"Here," Luna said, holding a mirror in front of me.

I'd never seen a more beautiful girl. I rubbed

my cheeks, relishing in the sight in the mirror and how bright my blue eyes shone. The last few times I glimpsed myself, it'd been in the broken mirror in my parent's room.

"You are definitely the prettiest prospect," Ara said, gently squeezing my shoulders.

"Prospect?"

Luna cleared her throat and nudged Ara. "Everything will be explained at dinner, my lady."

"Please, call me Rosalie," I said with a smile.

They both nodded.

"Now follow us, it's time to meet Lord Demious," Ara said.

Longingly, I glanced at the large fluffy bed. "Can't I rest for a bit?"

Two weeks locked in a wagon not only made every single muscle cry out for a soft place to rest, but all my energy had seeped out in the tub's warmth leaving me drained and tired.

"Lord Demious has crafted a wonderful feast," Ara said, gently ushering me toward the hallway.

Food. Real, hot, delicious food? No salted wafers or beef that had long passed its expiration? I could go to dinner for that. With a nod, and awkward stomach grumble, I followed the twins down the winding staircase to the main floor.

A butler dressed in a perfectly black tailored suit and matching bowtie opened a set of gold doors to the dining hall. There were ten other girls already sitting at the table in the banquet area. Each one uniquely beautiful, all of us human. The other girls sat quietly, staring at one another. We must have all been separated until now, but why? Examining all the girls, it occurred to me on what prospect might mean and I would rather be a slave.

When I had sold my freedom, it was under the assumption I'd be a servant in Lord Demious' home for a total of one year. One year, then I could return to home and hopefully this time with enough money to heal my firehawks. It was obvious the troll duped me, but into what and why? I had only shown him a tiny aspect of my magic. The flicker of a flame, strong enough to showcase my power, but not powerful enough that the magi would come after me.

One empty seat sat at the head of the table. I envisioned what Lord Demious would look like: fat, old, and full of dark evil secrets. The rumors spoke of him as being crazed and obsessed with magic. Eccentric and unmarried. A living nightmare who used his shadow magic to ensnare and seduce any who came too close. Then there were the stories of women going missing, nobles come for a grand party only to disappear by morning.

Working for Lord Demious was a risk, but I had no choice. I needed enough coin to pay off my debt to the bank and have enough to pay a healer from the Golden City. Not only were my firehawks weak, but because they couldn't hunt the plague snakes destroying the crops, the poison continued to spread through the rest of the North. I prayed to the All Father that one year wouldn't be too long to save my home.

I took a seat between a waif of a girl and a woman whose skin reminded me of the caramel candies my brother used to sneak to me at night. Her haunting sea-green eyes had even me hypnotized.

"Hi," I said to both. "I'm Rosalie."

The waif gaped at me with a wide-eyed stare. Her stark blonde hair and pale skin made her frail frame seem even more fragile than it ought to be.

"I don't think she speaks," said the beauty next to me. "I'm Janetta."

Janetta's chestnut wavy hair hung around her shoulders and almost grazed the bowl of soup when she leaned forward.

"Why are we all sitting in the hall, and did you all just arrive?" I had so many questions and needed someone to answer them. "What are we doing here?"

"I arrived yesterday." Janetta held her spoon right before her lips, as if savoring the sweet aroma.

Breaking a piece of bread off the roll on my plate, I dipped it into the soup bowl. "Why would a lord buy so many pretty slaves? Are we to be some obscene harem?"

Each passing moment I regretted giving myself in exchange to pay off my family's debt, but with my brother, Calvin, at war and our parents gone, someone had to save our home. The money Calvin left me had quickly run out. I had no more options. Desperation led me to that blasted troll at the market.

"I hear he's searching for a wife," Janetta whispered.

The banquet doors opened and a tall lean man with wavy brown hair and handsome chocolate eyes walked into the room. "Hello, ladies. I am Lord Demious. Welcome to my home."

Everyone said hello, but my voice caught in my throat when I noticed the figure standing next to our host.

A fae.

This was no high snooty city fae either. Fae were wild, raw, and commanding with coloring varying like a rainbow. They kept to their own and rarely concerned themselves with the other races. I'd never seen one up close. I don't think anyone I knew had ever seen one, and now, here one stood in all his rugged glory. He had short, shaggy silver hair that hung in his face and around his pointy ears, covering a portion of the most piercing light lavender eyes I'd ever seen. His velvety plum toned skin made his eyes too piercing to look at. The twin swords at his hips added to his powerful presence and the ivy tattoo crawling up his right arm perfectly added to his persona.

Demious must have sensed our curiosity, for I wasn't the only one gaping.

"This is the head of my guard, Baine. You will get used to him," Demious said before sitting.

Janetta and I stared at one another, trying to hide our shock.

Maybe fae were common in Farrow's Gate, but not from where I lived. I wasn't sure I could get used to him.

Dinner moved painfully slow while Demious ranted about his status and power and going on about his magical prowess and how he kept the darkthings from entering Farrow's Gate. He may have been more attractive if he wasn't so boorish. I found it hard to believe all the stories about him and his shadow magic . . . he seemed so *meh*.

I tried to be attentive, but my gaze shifted to the fae who stoically stared ahead. Not once did he look at any of the girls or seem interested in anything being discussed.

After the roasted quail had been served, I desperately needed to relieve myself. "Excuse me, my lord."

Lord Demious smiled at me. "Yes?"

"Is there a place I can refresh?"

"Of course, Baine, show her."

Baine's gaze met mine and there was nothing but contempt in those pretty eyes. I stood and followed him out of the hall.

Lord Demious must've been very powerful. How else could a fae be stuck in this estate with that snore of a lord? Baine should be out in the wilds, hunting, ravaging. If I was to be some prospect and not a servant, I'd need an ally, and who better than the male closest to Lord Demious.

"Here." Baine nodded at a door on our left.

But I couldn't move, not when his deep voice raked against my skin. He sounded as ancient as the old trees in the North, solid, deep.

"Is there a problem?"

"Forgive me," I said, using my polite voice, and gently bowed. "I have never met a fae before."

"I'm not here for your pleasure, go."

I ignored the slight and ran inside the washroom. Hiking up my dress, I used the toilet, then cleaned myself, making sure to pat the sweat off my brow and make myself presentable. I hadn't been forced to wear such a constricting outfit since I was sixteen. Lord Demious still hadn't explained why there were a bunch of women at dinner. I needed answers.

Exiting the washroom, Baine motioned for me to walk, and we returned to the hall where, *surprise*, Lord Demious was still discussing his latest accomplishment.

If I wasn't so hungry, I would have paid more attention to the magistrate, but my stomach couldn't seem to fill. Each decadent dish was more satisfying than the next until finally after dessert had been served, creampuffs and strawberries, I could barely stuff anymore in.

"I'm sure you're all curious as to why you are here."

My ears perked up and I listened. *Finally, something useful.*

He cleared his throat and continued. "I will choose one of you to be my wife. My bride must compliment me well in order to maintain the magic within Farrow's Gate. We will explore your abilities over these next few weeks. Each of you were chosen, but only one of you will be claimed. The rest of you will pay off the debts you owe over the next three years in an undisclosed location. You may explore the estate grounds during the day. Your collars will not let you go past the boundaries."

Not one girl spoke, half of us were barely breathing.

Was this a competition?

I came to pay off a debt, not be wed, and three years? The troll told me one. I couldn't be away from the farm that long. The old ranger watching the firehawks may not even live another three years, and my hawks were too sick, and had been since my parents died.

Three years wasn't an option for me.

Lord Demious smiled. "We'll start tomorrow."

Janetta and I shared a worried glance.

Without access to my flame, I had no choice but to play along, but I had no intention of being anyone's wife. What did Demious mean by saying undisclosed location? With each word my apprehension grew.

Something warned me that if I didn't marry Demious, I might never see my home again.

TWO

BAINE

Lord Demious headed to the drawing room, summoning his assistant, Alec, to his side. I kept my comments about his bridal competition to myself. It wasn't my concern on how the lord chose his bride, though I found the methods a bit odder than his usual antics.

"Alec," Lord Demious said as we entered. "I need the backgrounds of these girls, abilities, families, and unpleasantries."

I found a spot by the bookshelf to stand until this tedious review was completed. Instead of patrolling and securing the barrier around the grounds, I'd become his personal escort for the night—though the man needed none with his multiple layers of protection spells.

Each one of the women presented tonight wore a dampening collar. Even if they possessed great magic, there'd be no accessing it with that necklace on. The keys were locked away in Demious' laboratory and only he possessed the magical ability to unlock the collars with a flick of his wrist. Beyond his natural talent, the magistrate had a knack for crafting powerful magical items, and preferably ones only he could control.

Lord Demious sat in his high-back chair behind the desk and whirled his hand in a circle, opening a scrying portal in the center of the room. "Let's start with those three."

"Ahh, yes, the Haalow sisters." Alec began rifling through a stack of papers he held. "All three live here in Farrow's Gate city, family is noble, mostly dabble in arcane and illusionary spells."

"And why are all three here?" Lord Demious tapped his finger on the desk, clearly bored."

Alec's glasses slipped down his nose, and he pushed them back up. "It appears Mr. Haalow has a gambling problem and owes the bank quite a bit of coin. He hopes one of them might make a suitable bride."

"Very well, next." With a flick, Lord Demious

moved the image to a pair of girls, one of them being the redhead I'd escorted to the washroom.

"What do we know about this one?" Lord Demious slid forward on the desk, swiveling and repositioning the scryer until the woman's face and voluptuous breasts filled the image. He pinched his fingers, enlarging the woman's chest until he smirked and re-adjusted the image back to her face.

"Hmmm." Alec shuffled through the papers. "This one was a surprise?"

"A surprise?" I stepped forward, hand on my hilt. "You mean you did not acquire her yourself?"

Alec's face reddened. "Well, it's a bit of a strange story."

"Hold, Baine. Let's not slit any throats just yet." Lord Demious waved a finger at Alec to bring him the paper and began reading. "So, I'm paying for my brides now?"

With a toss, he flung the paper across the desk. "Explain."

"Yes, well, you had requested women with high magical talents, and one of our traders from the North heard. He managed to acquire Miss Rosalie Hawk and traded her for a reasonable sum."

"And why would I want to pay for a woman I may not even marry?"

The red in Alec's face deepened. "What we do know is her parents were both skilled in fire, natural sorcery, at extremely high levels, but passed the previous year—no reason listed. I believe . . . yes, here it is. She had agreed to serve one year of servitude in exchange for the deed to her family's farm and about a hundred gold coin. They breed firehawks."

Lord Demious rubbed his goatee, something he did when in deep thought. "Exceptional creatures. Does she know why she's here?"

"I believe she does now, my lord." Alec's eyes widened a bit and sweat glistened at his brow. "I will personally explain the misunderstanding and that if not chosen, we will uphold the one year as agreed."

"No."

"My lord," Alec said, his cheeks reddening to almost crimson.

"Let her believe she will either gain my favor or work the three years. Her deal was not with me."

"Of course, understood." Alec wiped his forehead. "Should we continue?"

"Proceed," Lord Demious said and switched the scrying image to another female.

The two went through the remaining girls, a waste of time. Alec seemed proud of acquiring such prospects, yet I couldn't find the meaning of the exercise. Lord Demious had enough power and wealth to marry any woman of his choosing. This "competition" seemed preposterous, even for him. Something else was at play here. After spending decades with the lord, I knew him well. I knew his true age, which would shock most people, and I knew that he did everything with perfect calculation. He had a reason for bringing all these females here and it wasn't to pick a bride.

I had tasks that needed to be completed before the night's end, and we had already spent two hours discussing magical talents and physical attributes with Alec pointing out which women appeared best suited for childbearing.

"My lord," I said, turning to the magistrate. "I need to patrol the grounds and check on the guards."

"You're excused." Lord Demious sighed as Alec began going over the schedule of events the women would be taking part in the following weeks.

Leaving, I headed out toward the main hall. Not only would I have to meet with my guards and remind them to leave these women alone, but if any of the prospects were harmed, I would have to answer for it.

We were accustomed to parties but having this many women on the estate for a prolonged time was reckless. Too much concentration of magic could attract darkthings, regardless of how impenetrable our defenses were. Those nightmarish shadow creatures were busy defiling the surrounding area by the Borderlands, but it was well known throughout all of Saol that the demons from the Rift in the Never were drawn to magic. Lord Demious had done a good job of keeping the barrier around Farrow's Gate intact, yet all this power in one area would not bode well.

Night had fallen and the halls of the estate held nothing but emptiness. As I turned to head to the kitchen, the soft click of a door caused me to stop. With slow movements, I stepped toward the large window in the hall and glanced outside.

Miss Hawk slipped out the front door in her nightgown.

Using my swiftness, I dashed to the entrance just as she stepped onto the cobbled garden path. What was she doing out here at night? And alone? While the grounds were constantly patrolled and the barrier kept out any powerful beings, it did not mean the area was completely safe.

With featherlight steps, I followed her.

The path she walked led to the stone waterfall pool near the orchid garden. A particularly beautiful section of the grounds that many visitors tended to flock to.

The human stood by the edge of the water. Moonlight shone through her sheer-white nightshift, highlighting every curve. Humming, she bent over slightly, playing with the water with her bare foot.

While Lord Demious allowed the guards to venture into town and get our fill, and sometimes even during parties, his prospects were not to be touched. This one would be trouble, which meant trouble for my men.

Quietly, I walked to her, silent and deadly.

Prospect or not, she would learn her place.

THREE

ROSALIE

The full moon lit the glittering pool on fire with starlight. Cautiously, I stepped forward and dipped my toe into the cool water. The water tickled my skin, and I swirled my foot around, holding my nightgown up with both hands. The cloud that enshrouded my mind inside had dissolved, leaving my thoughts clear.

What to do?

Would it be so bad to marry him?

Demious wasn't unattractive and he was wealthy. If I gained his trust, he may let me leave or have the farm taken care of in Calvin's absence. He certainly had the coin and power to help my firehawks. It was too soon to see if

Lord Demious was a kind man or the devious magistrate from the stories I'd heard. I'd need more information to know if he would help me, and if not, well, I'd have to find a way to escape, and quickly.

"You should not be out here."

Startled by the deep voice, I spun around, my foot slipping on the edge. I felt myself fall, but never hit the water.

"Why are you here?" Baine held my arm in a tight grip.

Shocked by his presence, I found it hard to speak. He yanked me forward and I placed both feet back on the ground. His eyes bore into me, and his stone face glared with annoyance.

"I needed some air."

Satisfied with my answer, he released me. "I suggest you return before someone sees you. Prospects are not allowed to wander at night."

I lowered my head, but only to stop from staring at him. "Just for a few moments, please?"

Baine growled and it sounded like a purr in my ear.

"Is that a no?" When I peeked up at him his lavender gaze sent my heart into a spiral.

"You humans are more stubborn than dwarves."

When he didn't drag me away, I took that as a yes. It was hard to think with Baine so close and untouchable, but I tried. Normally, I didn't act so foolish around men, but this was no man. He was something else, and I was an extremely curious thing.

I sat on the edge of the pool and dipped my legs in, whirling my feet around in the cool water. A cool breeze flew around me, pricking my skin. The trickling of the waterfall in the corner of the pool relaxed my body and my mind drifted to my flock.

There were so few of the firehawks left, and now they were in the care of a forgetful old ranger while I sat here in some ridiculous competition for a man I didn't even want.

Three years of service? That wasn't even an option. The plague snakes would continue their slithering path of destruction and soon the entire North would be in danger of starvation. If I wanted to save my home, I had to convince Lord Demious to help me or escape, and I wasn't sure which one would be the more difficult option.

Baine stood no more than twenty feet away, hands gripping the hilts of his swords. His jaw clenched so tightly I wondered if he was in pain. Using my long hair as a shield, I peeked over at the fae, admiring how the moonlight made the silver in his tattoo sparkle and how even with a scowl, he seemed like a dream.

When my guardian seemed more interested in the flowing wisteria across the arched lattice, I went back to my thoughts, thinking about my home and how I would get out of this disastrous situation.

Taking care of the farm alone had taken its toll on me and left me with nothing but the energy to dream, and my dreams ran wild with a life I couldn't have. There was so much of the world I wanted to see. Saol had wild plains filled with shifting beasts, magical sands that shimmered with various reds and pinks, and forests thick with fairies and glittering stars. How could someone who burned brighter than the sun sit still on a farm . . . but I had a duty, one I wouldn't ignore, but one day I would pass it on to someone else and get my grand adventure.

A screech tore through the sky, followed by another.

"Move," Baine ordered, brandishing his matching short swords.

Though I heard his command, my gaze focused on the streak of red and orange flying at me, swirling in and out of the sky like colored lightning. A dance of fire that sang to my wild heart.

Ash raptors.

When I was a little girl, my father told me

stories of the magnificent beasts that flew around high cliffs and left a trail of fire in their wake. The group of them streaked across the blue sky.

I clawed at the collar on my neck, desperate to free my flame. Even with the magical dampener plunging my power into darkness, a tiny warmth bloomed in my chest at the sight of the flames trailing behind the raptors.

Baine yanked me to my feet and shoved me behind him. "Get down."

"Don't provoke them!"

Other humans may have feared the screeches and vivid lights, but not me. My heart soared at the idea of seeing an ash raptor, birds of prey that were born of fire and magic. My hawks were chicklets compared to these majestic creatures.

Three swooped in, sunset feathers coating their bodies.

Baine readied his swords, feet sliding into a fighting stance.

Palms up, I stilled, knowing any sharp movements could cause an unwarranted attack. If ash raptors were anything like my firehawks they would be curious, but not naturally aggressive.

Easy. Calm and collected just like Father taught me.

"Don't move," I hissed, urging the fae beside me not to raise his swords.

The larger one with a plume of blood red feathers reached out and plucked me off the grass. I squeaked, or screamed, I wasn't sure exactly what type of noise I made, but I wasn't thinking the birds would take me into the air. "Baine!"

He glanced up, frowned, and sheathed his swords. When he didn't immediately call for help, I panicked. Then with a shake of his head, he ran.

The birds flew into the sky, zigzagging around the treetops, and making my head spin. When my father taught me about all the fire creatures in our world, he weaved magnificent stories about how we were connected through the elements, ours being fire. Without access to my flame, I had no way of controlling these raptors like I did my hawks.

My father also forgot to mention how deadly the raptor's talons were.

Sharp claws dug into and under my shoulders where the raptor carried me, nicking my skin.

"Put me down," I said gently, attempting to coax the beast, but it didn't respond, only flew farther away from the mansion.

The estate had miles and miles of land; it would take me hours to get back to the mansion if those raptors even dropped me.

Where in all of Saol are these creatures

taking me?

Higher and higher we flew, my head getting hazy. Reaching up, I gripped the legs, hoping I could control the flight, but with a wingspan of at least twelve feet, my nudging did little to deter the creature. The raptors screeched at one another in a beautiful symphony, and if I wasn't terrified about crashing to my death, I may have enjoyed the melody. The wind blew my hair as we rode on the breeze, dipping into it. I used to watch my flock zipping through the sky and had always yearned for that same wild freedom.

How different it seemed having it.

The mansion shrunk in the growing distance.

A bolt of lightning shocked my body and I screamed as we slammed into an invisible barrier. The collar buzzed, shooting pain down my neck and spine. The raptors went into a frenzy into the wall again, making me almost bite my lip in pain. The one carrying me dove lower to the ground and each time it neared the wall, electricity burned through my mind, my body, through everything.

"Stop! Please! Put me down," I wailed, pleading with the bird to set me free.

As if sensing my pain, the raptor released me . . . ten feet from the ground.

I tried to land and roll, but my left foot rolled under me, shooting pain up my leg. "Ahh."

Pushing against the dirt, I sat and examined my foot, touching the puffy part of my ankle. With a wince, I used my good leg and slowly stood. After tending the farm by myself for so long, being alone didn't frighten me, and I'd had quite a few injuries I had to take care of all by myself. It might take me a day or two to find my way, but I'd eventually make it back to the mansion, somehow.

Swaying, I held out my arms, balancing myself, every muscle aching. There was one thing I did learn today: I was not escaping the estate. Not with this collar on.

The trees directly in front of me rustled. Holding my breath, I waited, fear forcing me to pull on the magical noose around my neck.

There was a *swoosh* to my right and a massive dire wolf stalked forward.

The creature must've been three hundred pounds, much larger than any normal wolf. It growled, revealing massive fangs dripping with saliva. Its silver hair seemed to reflect the moonlight, making it shine.

"Nice wolf." I hobbled back, biting my lip as my ankle throbbed. I pulled at the collar keeping my powers in check. "Ugh. Why won't this thing come off?"

The beast stopped growling and lowered its head.

And began shifting.

I fell back on to the ground, scurrying as best I could from the beast in front of me. The fur disappeared, replaced with smooth skin, and then Baine was on one knee, gazing at me with furious intent.

"You're . . ." My heart raced so fast I couldn't speak. "You're . . ."

"A shapeshifter. I know what I am."

Impossible.

If fae were the fairy tale you heard about, shapeshifters were the nightmare that came and visited. From what I knew, not all fae could shapeshift, only the extremely powerful ones, including the immortal King of the Fae, Kane. He was a polymorph, and I'd heard he would judge his people in different forms based on his mood.

How did Lord Demious end up with a shifter fae as his bodyguard?

Needing to distract myself from the terror before me, I changed the topic. "How did you find me so fast?"

"We all have our secrets." Baine glanced down. "Are you hurt?"

"It's my foot."

"Let me see."

I stretched out my bad leg and he picked up my foot, gently pressing the sides.

"Does this hurt," he asked as he pressed.

"No, no, ouch!" I jerked back.

"You'll need to rest. It's not sprained, only a little bruised. You'll feel better tomorrow, but no walking on it tonight."

"What does that mean?"

He took one of his blades out of its sheath and grabbed my dress. "I'll have to carry you."

"The whole way?"

"Yes," he replied and sliced a piece of my nightgown off. "You were foolish to stand there. What were you thinking?"

"I didn't think they were going to whisk me off into the sky. I think they wanted to help. They tried bringing me through the barrier, which really hurt."

Baine lifted my leg and my nightshift slid toward my hips. The night breeze blew through me and while my skin prickled with sensitivity where he touched, his gaze focused on wrapping my foot.

"That should help until we have a cleric examine it."

This time, Baine looked directly at me. His face pinched in that angry stare, before his gaze went to my mouth, and he wiped the blood off with a swipe of his finger. "What are you?"

"I'm human."

"No, you're something else." He lifted his left

hand and whispered in the fae tongue. His tattoo glowed a vibrant silver, tiny tendrils of magic hovering over his arm.

He brought his palm to my body, slowly hovering over the skin, so close I could feel the tinge of magic seeping through my night dress. Inch by inch he trailed his hand around me. When he hovered by my breasts, my pounding heart almost made me faint. I stilled, not knowing what else to do.

His jaw twitched, but he kept moving, circling around until he stopped by my heart. His eyes widened and he pressed his palm to my breast. Too anxious to move or speak, I stared at him, wondering the point of this odd exercise.

Clinical like a doctor, his touch had no sensuality, no hint at a playful tussle.

The glowing stopped and he pulled his hand away. "Your magic is wild, strong. There is something old inside you."

Father made me and my brother swear to never to speak of our heritage. We pretended to be a family descended from sorcerers. If anyone knew that my father had been half human and half elemental, the Magi Council would have stolen my brother and me the day we were born. The elementals were the only uncontrolled race in Saol. Also, the oldest and strongest magic users.

"Just plain old magic," I said with a wide smile.

Baine's gaze penetrated my common sense and I almost told him the truth. "Lie to me all you want, human, but Lord Demious will learn, and I suggest you be honest."

Without giving me a proper moment to argue, Baine swept me into his arms. "Close your eyes and hold on. This will be uncomfortable for you."

Like a winter gale, Baine shot through the woods, moving so fast I couldn't focus on our surroundings. I squeezed my eyes shut and clutched his neck while he held me tightly to his chest.

He was the rustle I heard, quick, deadly, unseen. Any creature that moved faster than the wind had come from deep magic, wild like mine. His scent reminded me of the dewy air right by a waterfall, crisp, clean, refreshing. With my head pressed against his chest, I inhaled the delicious aroma and captured it for my dreams later.

I don't know how long he ran for, but when he stopped, my head didn't.

"Ugh. I feel sick." I gripped my temples.

"This is the uncomfortable part. I would've had you ride me in my wolf form, but that is not a smooth ride, and your ankle may have been agitated. This was the best solution." He gently set me on the grass where I vomited, not once, but twice.

"Here." With an arm around my waist, he helped me stand and walk over to the fountain. "Drink."

I leaned over and drank the cool water, not caring it drenched the front of my clothes or my face.

"That was more than uncomfortable." I relaxed against him and wiped my mouth. "Can we please rest for a minute?"

Baine nodded, jaw clenched, his fingers gently pressed against my hip. I glanced down and saw why: my dress covered absolutely nothing thanks to the water.

Covering myself with my arms, I said, "Thank you for coming for me."

"I am the head of the guard. It's my duty."

We were back by the marble pool, hidden from all eyes, surrounded by the sweetest smelling peonies in all the lands. Baine set me down on the nearby bench while he stood.

My thoughts went to the fae beside me. I had so many questions about him, and his people, if he knew any other fae that could shapeshift like him. Some of the races were biased against others, and hybrids were considered shameful. There were rumors inbreeding decreased magical abilities, and to a point it did, but then there were people like my twin and me where the unique hybrid became something else.

Needing to break the silence, I decided to see how much Baine was willing to share. "How long have you been Lord Demious' bodyguard?"

Baine's mouth curved into a frown.

"Not a small talker, I see." I sighed.

If I thought winning this dark beauty to my side would be easy, I was wrong. Fae were supposed to be full of passion, danger, and alpha personalities to rival the great grizzlies, but this one couldn't even hold a conversation.

"If you've regained your composure, you need to return to your room." Without waiting for an answer, he scooped me up in his arms and began walking.

"Hey!" I squeaked as his rough hands gripped me tight.

"Lord Demious will need to learn about the raptors."

This close I could see tiny flecks of pink in his lavender eyes. Pink. A color so far removed from this fae's façade.

"And the rest?" I asked while placing a hand on his chest.

"He only needs to know what happened with the raptors, not that you provoked them."

Baine could pretend he wasn't attracted to me, but the fast beat of his heart told me something else. If I could win over this fae, and escape, not only would my home be saved, but

I would have a powerful ally who could help me bring my brother back home from war.

I just had to figure out how to seduce a fae.

FOUR

ROSALIE

The next morning the twins dressed me in a tight-fitting bodice that once again displayed more of me than I cared for. I moved my ankle in a circle, and thankfully there was no pain. I'd always seemed to heal a bit faster than normal humans.

"Why am I the only woman with her breasts hanging over the butter dish?" I groaned to Janetta at breakfast.

She smiled and glanced down. "Probably because you're the only one with breasts that large."

True, while all the women here had their own beautiful quality, I seemed to be the curvy girl out of the bunch. "What do you think will happen today?"

"I don't know. It feels odd to be competing for *his* hand."

We both glanced at Lord Demious who sat at the head of the long table, cutting his biscuit with a knife . . . who does such a weird thing? He wasn't unattractive, and he did have a warm sweetness to those chocolate eyes, but how was any woman here supposed to focus on Demious with Baine wearing those black leathers?

Baine leaned against the wall behind Lord Demious, arms folded, gaze absolutely avoiding me.

His swords hung at his hips and there was something very alluring about the way he rested one leg over the other, seeming both relaxed and deadly at the same time.

"Good morning, ladies!" Demious said with a smile, breaking my concentration on the male behind him. "I hope last night you all rested well. Today, you'll meet with our scribe Jasper and review what languages you can speak and write in."

Demious stood and dabbed a napkin to his mouth. "Tonight, we shall meet in the ballroom where you can enjoy each other's company. Even though this is a competition, you should all get along."

When Demious smiled at all of us, the gesture

didn't reach his eyes. Why would someone as powerful as him even need a competition? This whole thing was ridiculous and unnecessary.

"Until tonight, my ladies." He bowed and left the dining hall, Baine following.

"I can't write."

Janetta and I both turned to the waif next to us. I still didn't know her name.

"I'm sure there are girls here who can't either, don't worry." I gave her a smile. "I'm Rosalie and this is Janetta. You can stay by us if you want."

She tilted her head at me. "Alicia."

"Hi, Alicia," Janetta said.

A tall older woman wearing a very tight bun and plain brown dress, came in clapping her hands. "Ladies, we will be moving to the library. Stay in line."

With a silent groan, I stood up. The bodice I wore seemed to crush against my chest even more with all the food I'd eaten. While I loved the soft red gown and the amber ruffles along the hem, it made it impossible to breathe. I hadn't worn a corset like this in years. There was no need to dress fancy when you spent most of the time in the dirt and chasing after a flock of fire hungry birds.

We followed the woman out into the hallway in a two-by-two formation deeper into the mansion, corridor after corridor, some with swirling marble walls, some with black velvet trimmed walls. Opulence decorated the halls of the mansion with gold molding and lavish furnishings made of the finest wood. Each time I trailed the rooms of this lavish estate, I noticed little eccentric entities. Like the massive golden statue of a scepter with shining eyes of a viper or how sometimes when I stared at the paintings really hard, the colors shifted, the image blending into another, and one not as peaceful as the meadow scene it portrayed.

Unlike most humans, my senses were heightened, and right now they warned me that the lord of this mansion wasn't the boorish man he appeared to be.

We entered into a beautiful library with mahogany desks, plenty of seating and a second floor of books that I could get lost in for days.

"I am head mistress Begalia," the woman said with pride. "I look over Lord Demious' estate. This estate has been in his family for over eleven generations."

"Can you believe one of us will get to live here?" Janetta whispered to me.

How could I tell her that was the opposite of what I wanted? I didn't come here to be a bride. My brother would throw a fit if he found out I'd sold myself off into servitude.

Just thinking of Calvin brought me to tears.

He left exactly six months after our parents died. Six months.

Father had always been the one to maintain the hawks, and with him gone, we only had our local ranger to assist in their healing. In the North, where red mountains and rushing rivers created one of the most majestic territories in all of Saol, we had one hindrance: plague snakes. Slimy reptiles invading from the swamps of the South. The firehawks hunted these creatures, stopping them from defiling the crops, but with the hawks weak and sick, the land was in dire need of aid.

Calvin thought fighting at the Borderlands would supply enough coin to pay what we owed to the bank and send for a healer from the Golden City. The center of Saol, and the one place with the top alchemists, healers, and priestesses. Someone there would know what was happening.

I begged Calvin not to go.

That was almost a year ago.

Ms. Begalia clapped again, releasing me from my thoughts. Her tight bun seemed to pull extra hard on her already sharp features. “You will each take a seat and draft a letter explaining your qualities and why you should be chosen.”

“She can’t be serious,” I said to Janetta as we sat at one of the tables.

Quill and ink had been left out, along with parchment. I glanced at the other girls, wondering if I was the only one who thought this charade was ridiculous. Three brunettes congregated at a table down from us. They all had the same slender nose and pale blue eyes.

"Those are the Haalow sisters," Janetta whispered while dipping her quill into the ink. "Claudia, Corella, and Chloe."

"Why are they all here?"

Janetta squinted at the girls. "They're in the room next to mine, and loud. I think they all have different abilities and expect Lord Demious will choose one. If he picks one, all three are saved. I think they're going for a package deal."

I could understand banding together. They couldn't be more than a few years apart with the youngest around sixteen—she was the youngest here, besides Alicia who I guessed couldn't be more than seventeen.

None of them were an old hag like me . . . twenty-two years old with no husband in sight. Some even thought I was too old to marry. It never bothered me, though. Sure, what woman didn't want a handsome man to roll around in the dirt with? Except, I didn't have *time* to roll around in the dirt unless I was chasing the chickens.

"I think it's nice they're protecting each other," I said with a sigh. "Better they work together."

Ms. Begalia slammed a wand on our table.

Janetta and I both jumped.

"There is no talking while you are writing." The head mistress frowned at us. "Proper ladies listen."

"Sorry," Janetta mumbled.

I couldn't say a word because the mole on Ms. Begalia's upper lip had a hair in it. A really long one. How could she leave it hanging like that? Did she not feel it when she washed her face? Did she like having a long black hair floating on the afternoon breeze?

"Is there a problem, Miss Hawk?" If Ms. Begalia frowned anymore her face would fall off.

Janetta bumped my thigh with her leg under the table, eyeing me to answer.

"No, ma'am." Quickly, I began scribbling on the parchment.

This is ridiculous.

Somehow, I managed to write about my hardiness, my tenacity, my fire magic—though, I left out the bigger details of that—and how grateful I would be to be chosen. Blah, blah, blah.

Mole maid came for our parchments and rolled them up. "Your next test will be outside. Follow me."

The ever-quiet Alicia, Janetta, and I followed the rest of the girls out through the doors and to a grassy field on the opposite side of the mansion where a line of circular targets had been set up.

Baine stood off to the side, arms crossed. Our gazes met and while my cheeks flooded with heat from his penetrating stare, his brooding expression glowered.

Was I that intolerable that he couldn't even say hello?

Ms. Begalia picked up a long bow from the tables in front of us. "As the lady of Farrow's Gate, you must be able to defend yourself and others."

She grabbed an arrow from a wicker basket and slung it on the bow. "Each of you will aim at the target like this, and release."

The arrow whizzed through the air, stabbing the red circle on the wood. A perfect bull's-eye.

"Ms. Begalia." One of the Haalow sisters raised her hand, maybe the middle one.

"Yes, Corella."

"What if you've never been taught how to use a bow?"

"Then you will learn today. You cannot always count on magic to save you. Begin!"

Janetta grabbed the shaft of an arrow. With the poise of a swan, Janetta lined up her shot, and . . . *thunk*. She turned at me, beaming.

"Show off," I grumbled and took one of the feathered arrows out of the basket. I cringed at the idea of showcasing my horribly inept archery skills. I already knew how horrible a shot I was and really didn't feel like sharing that truth. I tugged back on the bowstring, feeling the tension, and squinting at the red dot thirty feet away. *One . . . two . . .*

Not only did the arrow not hit the target, but it also flopped and barely made it a foot.

Giggles came from my left. Apparently, most of the girls had some basic archery skills. With the tear in the Rift between the Borderlands growing, everyone in Saol had to be prepared. The darkthings fed off magical energy, and sometimes a magical arrow or sword in the right spot would end them faster than a blast from a lightning bolt, but being born of fire, I didn't need a weapon.

I was one.

If they knew about my heritage, no one would be laughing at me.

"Keep trying," Janetta said as Alicia shot her bow and came within inches of hitting her mark.

"Yeah." I sighed and grabbed another arrow.

Taking a deep breath, I lined it up, switching between closing my left and right eye to see which one made the shot easier, which was neither.

"Your form is wrong." Baine's sudden appearance made me jump and I shot the arrow, miserably.

"Thanks, that was extremely helpful," I groaned and swung around to face him. "Don't sneak up on people. It's rude."

Sunlight hit those lavender eyes of his and he damn near sparkled.

"Do you want the help," he said evenly, "or do you prefer to continue to fail?"

My chest heaved with fury. "I don't need any help. I'll figure it out."

We glared at one another, and he stepped closer until his whisper could only be heard by me. "You lack the skill to do so."

If Baine wasn't Lord Demious' pet lackey, I would've had more than one choice word for him. Instead, I ignored the slight and kept my mouth shut. If Baine wanted to help, he had an odd way of showing it.

"I'll take some help." One of the sisters sauntered up to Baine and I quickly stepped back, examining my bow. She placed a hand on his bicep.

He glanced down at her hand then back up at her face. "Very well."

"I'm Claudia," she said with a smile. "It's so nice to meet you."

They stepped away and as they did, I wished I could burn the smirk right off Baine's face.

FIVE

BAINE

Reaching the guard house, I did one final check on the security for the night. Anytime Lord Demious invited the nobles over for a ball or other ostentatious occasion, my men wasted time saving the fools from getting lost in the garden maze or wandering to areas of the estate that were off limits.

Having a group of women to babysit didn't make my task easier. When Lord Demious had mentioned this soiree of his, I suggested he focus on picking a bride and not playing with the nobles. At almost every festivity he had, I would need to send the ladies home, discreetly, the next day. The magistrate had a large appetite for many things, including women.

"You three will stay in the ballroom," I said to my men. "The rest, normal duties."

"Yes, captain." My first, Marco, another fae, motioned for the two guards to go ahead. Once they were far enough away, he pulled me aside.

"What is Demious doing?" Marco never used proper titles when dealing with the eccentric lord. "Those raptors showing up signal a magic disturbance, and he's done nothing but plan a party for a bunch of females?"

Marco rubbed the back of his shaved head. "Something is off."

"Keep your head about you. As long as the barrier around the estate holds, there should be no more creatures entering."

"You sense it, don't you? It's as if my body is singing with magical energy with all these prospects in one area."

"I do." Though I trusted Marco with my life, I would not tell him about my own conclusions, not until I had more information.

"I want to show you something." Marco motioned for me to follow him out the back entrance and toward the stables. "It may be nothing, but after the incident with the raptors, we need to be sure."

The private stables held only Lord Demious' horses, a mix of work horses and riding ones.

Marco stopped at the first gate. "I noticed it this morning when she wouldn't eat."

A white mare lay on her side. An odd black marking skittered along her neck from a spot by her ear. I squatted by the animal, and she snorted.

"Shh. Easy." I ran my hand along her smooth mane.

"What do you think it is?"

"I'm not sure." Activating my tattoo, I sent a magical pulse through my palm, searching for the source of entry.

As Lord Demious' head guard, he had crafted the tattoo as a means for me to verify magical properties, whether it be on an object or person. The tattoo heated as I reached an area underneath the mare's ear.

"Here." I pointed to a puncture made by four holes in a circular shape.

Marco leaned over. "What type of creature would cause such a wound?"

"I'm not sure. Has Lord Demious seen this?" I patted the mare before standing and exiting the stall.

"Not yet. I was only informed a little while ago."

Farrow's Gate had been an epicenter for magical oddities and creatures. Besides Lord Demious, there were many mages in the town, keeping watch to make sure any dangerous monsters were dealt with swiftly.

"Where did you find her?" I asked.

"Grazing with the others."

"Show me."

We exited the stables and I followed Marco toward the open area . . . right where the females had been practicing archery. "This is not good."

"I know," Marco grumbled.

Already my mind began calculating possibilities. Did one of the females summon something? Were the dampeners not working?

Lighting the tattoo, I waved my palm over the grounds, walking slowly. Whatever happened to appear and attack the mare had long gone.

"I'll let Lord Demious know," I said. "Do a barrier check and report back anything you find."

Marco sighed. "Aye aye."

We split directions, me returning to where Lord Demious entertained the guests. Carriages and horses filled the wide circle in front of the mansion. Lord Demious tended to show off to the nobles during his gatherings, though he hardly needed to. His magic kept the more dangerous creatures away from Farrow's Gate which made the incident with the raptors unusual.

I thought back to Miss Hawk and how the beasts tried taking her. There was something ancient about the magic I sensed in the human. Even dulled by the dampener, it had a raw edge to it. She hadn't shown much promise at archery, but that did little to discredit the rest of her.

I'd reached the ballroom as the quartet began playing. I searched for Lord Demious who sat at the head of the table, drinking, and speaking with Alec. A spread of meats and cheese before him. The female prospects hadn't entered the room yet.

"My lord," I said, interrupting the conversation. "I need to show you something."

"Whatever it is, it will wait." Lord Demious smiled at a human female who curtsied as she passed.

"I don't think this can," I said with a bit more urgency.

"Is someone dying? Has someone come to murder me at my own party?"

"No."

"Then it'll wait." Lord Demious picked up a goblet of wine. "Drink, your stuffiness is ruining my mood."

"Of course, my lord." I took the goblet and downed it in three gulps.

Lord Demious grinned and took the decanter from the table. "There are many beautiful women here tonight. Find a noble that suits you and have some fun."

It was no surprise Lord Demious treated me differently than the other guards. While the others had been hired, I hadn't. I stayed out of loyalty. I owed Lord Demious a life debt. One I didn't think I'd ever be able to repay.

"As the head of your guard, it's my duty not to have fun."

He laughed and clapped a hand to my shoulder. "You are also my friend and I hate to see you sulk. Sit with me for a moment."

While the world thought of Demious as an evil, twisted man, he wasn't always. Demious wanted everyone to fear him, though the ones closest to him never did, and only because he fiercely protected his own.

"Why are you doing this?" I asked, taking the empty seat beside him. "With your stature, you could have any of these women."

Keeping his gaze on the nobles that passed, he smiled. "My line needs power. Tell me, who do you think I should pick?"

"We haven't seen what the women are capable of."

Demious filled my goblet again and nodded for me to drink, something I rarely did, but Lord Demious pushed me to. He must've been on edge.

"True," he said. "But if I had to choose,

which one?"

My mind went to the human girl with vibrant red hair, but for reasons unknown to me, I didn't say her name. "What do I know of human women? They're all the same to me."

Lord Demious held up his goblet with a grin. "If I didn't need you, I'd send you away to find a nice fae female and have lots of wolf babies."

I frowned at the absurdity of the sentiment. Family was not in my future. I was a blade, nothing more.

The grin left Lord Demious' face. "One day you will find someone worth leaving me for. Now go, your frown is ruining my mood."

Taking my leave, I thought on what he said. The idea of finding a mate left the moment my own family exiled me. My place was here, and nothing or no one would change my mind.

SIX

ROSALIE

"Do I really need to wear this? It's impossible to move in." I twisted to see the furry tail attached to the auburn tulle of my dress, just above my backside.

"Lord Demious has required each of the ladies to represent an animal, for fun." Ara smiled.

I groaned and grabbed the sides of my dress. "And I'm a fox?"

Luna entered the room carrying a white and red fur shawl. "You should be honored that Lord Demious has invited other nobles tonight."

After two days, I could tell the twins apart by the scowl that always seemed to be on Luna's face. It was the only defining feature between them.

If it wasn't for the long furry tail, I'd look gorgeous. Ara did a fantastic job of braiding the top of my hair and leaving the rest to hang around my bare shoulders. The dress cinched my waist, but didn't smother me, and while my ladies were out there prominently in the sweetheart gown, they weren't popping out like before.

A bell chimed through the estate.

"It's time!" Ara grabbed the shawl from Luna and draped it across my shoulders.

"It's summer," I whined.

"Only wear it for your entrance."

My stomach fluttered with nerves. I could handle one odd lord, but a whole room of nobles? I had never been to any type of court. Not that I cared what these nobles thought, but still. I didn't want to come across as an imbecile or embarrass myself, especially in front of that trio of sisters.

We filed into the hallway where the other girls and their maids followed. Two doors down, a girl dressed in all white with feathers lining the dress stepped out in front of me. She was more poised and elegant than I ever could be.

The ballroom was on the first floor past the dining hall. My stomach grumbled thinking of dinner and hoping Demious would feed us soon. Lunch had been nothing but cucumber-dill finger sandwiches and pomegranates. A meal like that couldn't sustain anyone for long.

"Rosalie!" Janetta waved at me from the head of a line of the other girls. Her brown hair hung in luscious curls and her hunter green dress brought out the hue of her exotic eyes.

We clasped hands and smiled at each other.

"You look gorgeous," we both said at the same time, and laughed.

"How are any of us going to compete with you," Janetta said with a pout.

"Have you seen yourself? You make a stunning frog."

"Ha! Frog? Is that what I'm supposed to be?"

"Ladies!" Ms. Begalia clapped, calling us to attention. "Listen well. You will be called in by name. When you are called, enter and take a seat at the head table near the front."

Ms. Begalia gave us a stern glare and Janetta skipped back to her place in line.

"Have fun tonight," Ara said.

"And don't get in trouble," Luna added.

All the maids left leaving us to stand there. The C-sisters, since their names all began with C, were first in line. Each one wore the distinct colors of the great cats, the oldest in black, the middle in a warm yellow, and the youngest in a mousy brown.

A male servant opened the door to the ball and called the first girl, then a few minutes later the next, and so on. I noticed that Alicia wasn't here. She was quiet, but why would she be excluded from this?

None of us had discussed our magical abilities or displayed any. I wondered what her secret gift was.

"Rosalie Hawk."

Though I heard my name, I couldn't find the nerve to move.

Until someone nudged me from behind—Ms. Begalia, of course.

Holding my hands in front of me, clasped together, I stepped into the hall.

My heart hammered at the room full of women too beautifully dressed and adorned with glittering jewelry and the men who whispered beside them. At the far end of the room, Lord Demious sat at the table, a grin on his face as he sipped from a golden goblet.

Each of the girls had taken a seat, leaving the last one on the end for me.

I refused to make eye contact with anyone, and my heart dropped a bit when I didn't see a certain fae. Shouldn't he be with Lord Demious? Baine was the head of Lord Demious' guard. Why wouldn't he be here? Tonight would've been the perfect opportunity to get to know the magistrate's trusted man a bit better.

Once I sat, the quartet in the corner began

playing and chatter filled the room. The girl next to me ignored me, speaking only to the girl on her right.

Thankfully, the table had wine.

A servant filled my goblet, and I guzzled the sweet and slightly dry liquid. It warmed my belly.

I can't remember the last time I had such a delicious drink.

Red and yellow chrysanthemum decorated the lavish table, which held a variety of honey fruits, cheese wheels, and salted pieces of meat that made my stomach roar with hunger. I grabbed a leg of quail and bit into the juicy meat.

If marrying Lord Demious meant eating this rich every night, well, I just might be persuaded. On the farm, we had simple treats, salted jerky, fresh apples, butter mixed with honey, and too much salt, but none of it compared to the feast in front of me.

The sisters hovered near Demious, who smiled and whispered to them.

Chewing, I wondered why the rumors of him spun such tall tales. He seemed the opposite of dark and dangerous. Eccentric, maybe, mysterious? Not so much.

Unless it's all a ruse.

Regardless of rumors and village gossip, there was no one as magically gifted in Farrow's

Gate as Lord Demious. He alone kept the wild magic at bay.

I grabbed another leg of quail, after noticing the girl beside me had barely touched any of the food surrounding her and devoured the succulent meat. These other women could be dainty, but not me. My magic tended to give me a ravenous appetite.

"Another glass, my lady?" The male servant from before brought the pitcher of wine over.

He had a kind, young face, with short blond curls a girl would die for. I held up the goblet. "Always, another, in fact, come back soon."

He smiled and I winked at him.

"I will make sure my lady has all the wine she requires." His bright smile faded as he looked up and past me. "Sorry, I'll return when you need me."

He scurried off and I followed his line of sight.

Baine.

If those eyes of his could speak, they'd probably be lecturing me on proper etiquette. I met his hard stare, raised my goblet, and in three sips drank it all.

I slammed the goblet on the table and wiped my lips with the back of my hand.

Baine frowned, clearly not impressed with my drinking ability.

The tempo of music increased, and nobles

filled the center of the dance floor, lining up. I loved to dance, but not with this ridiculous tail on my butt. I twisted and undid the safety pin and shoved the furry object under my seat.

With an excited grin, I stood and glanced around. None of the other girls tried to get up. Were we not allowed?

I bounced on the heels of my feet as the beat began to drum in my soul. Though my flame hid in darkness, the spark still lived, desperate to ignite the night.

Lord Demious' gaze found mine. He nodded at me, smiling.

Thank you, I mouthed and quickly found a spot in the line.

A young noble with a red hat bowed across from me. I curtsied.

And then the music seized me.

With a flourish, the ladies met their partners across the line. My man hooked his arm around mine, smiling, and we twirled around the dance floor, switching off partners on the next crescendo. My heart soared and my flame flickered inside, lighting my steps.

Another swing and I linked arms with a burly man who hooted and had reddened cheeks. I laughed and he swirled me around right into Lord Demious' embrace.

"I'm glad you're enjoying yourself," he said,

taking my hand in his.

I laughed and smiled. "I love to dance."

"I see." He motioned to the door leading out to the gardens. "Walk with me."

We left the dance floor, arm in arm, my heart pounding and sweat dotting my brow. The sisters all glared at me as we passed, and I felt a bit of pride knowing that Lord Demious chose me for a stroll and not one of them.

Baine followed us outside, and the racing in my heart from dancing only intensified. The setting sun turned the sky into a rainbow of soft pinks and lilac, just like Baine's eyes. Farrow's Gate seeped with magical energy, and it bled into the sky like a shooting star.

Cascades of fragrant, purple-hued wisteria crawled along the wooden archway that covered the stone path we walked. The hanging flowers were a feast to both the eyes and nose. Even someone like Lord Demious could seem beautiful in this picturesque scene.

"Tell me," Demious said. "Did you know why you were coming to my estate?"

"I thought to work, that's what the troll said."

"Hmm." Demious pursed his thin lips. "You must've shown him something special to be offered a chance to be my bride."

I couldn't tell Demious the truth, not the whole truth at least. "I dabble in the arts."

Demious laughed and patted my hand. "I would very much like to see."

This was my one chance to find out if I could really leave this place or not. "I'll happily show you, if you could answer one of my questions."

"Go on," he said, keeping his arm looped with mine.

"The troll said nothing about a bridal competition, and while I understand how great an honor it would be, my firehawks need me. I won't abandon them."

He stopped us by the garden maze near the pool and faced me. "I admire a woman who can speak freely. Know this, if you do become my wife, not only will I re-unite you with your flock, but I'll bring them here where they will thrive in Farrow's Gate."

"No."

"No?" Lord Demious eyed me, a darkness clouding over his gaze. The change in demeanor sent a chill through my body as his grip on my arm tightened.

"I am from the North. If you know about firehawks, you know the role they play in the plague happening there."

Suddenly, the boorish, plain man disappeared, and shadows surrounded his body. I stepped back, trying to pull away. My gaze flitted to Baine who stood still, gaze on his master.

"Do not speak to me as if I am a common man," Lord Demious growled.

"I meant no offense." My heart hammered as Lord Demious dug his fingers into my skin.

Shadows seeped out from his body, curling and sliding around mine. I stilled, eyes widening as Lord Demious smiled. "Know this, if you want to save your little birds, you will impress me or you will be shipped off."

Heat swirled in my core. I'd never taken threats well. "I am not a child, and I have fought bigger beasts than you."

His eyes shifted to black.

Lord Demious yanked me forward, pressing his fingers into my waist. Opening his mouth, a stream of black mist expelled. He blew the shadows over my face, inserting them up my nostrils. I coughed on the thick mist, gasping for air.

"This is your only warning," he said, his voice scratchy and rough. "Do not threaten me, ever again."

"My lord," Baine said, shifting to stand beside me. "I suggest you move to a more private location if you wish to continue this conversation. There are nobles nearby."

The shadows receded, and Lord Demious smiled. "Of course. Where are my manners. "Let us walk."

I didn't want to go anywhere with this man.

His hand on my arm made me shiver with fear, and I desperately needed to be free of his grip. Trembling, I focused on holding back the tears, feeling helpless without my flame to protect me.

"I am not an evil man, Miss Hawk. My wife will be an equal to me."

His words did nothing to remove the vileness of feeling his magic crawl up my nose. I wanted to bathe and let hot steam flush out his lingering stench.

"Lord Demious!" A huffing servant, the one who attended me inside, came running. "Your presence is required in the drawing room. Lord Harrington and the others have arrived."

"I'll be right there. Tell them to wait." Demious took my hand, his fake smile widening. "You may enjoy the gardens. When you're finished, Baine will see you back to the ballroom."

He planted a kiss on my fingers, the touch sending a wave of nausea through me. "Good night, Rosalie. I expect us to have more time together, tomorrow."

Once Demious had ventured far enough away, I turned and walked toward the garden maze, desperate for privacy and a moment to think.

"Where do you think you're going?" Baine grabbed my arm.

I turned and stared at the hand holding me in place.

"For a walk." With a tug, I ripped my arm out of Baine's grasp and picked up my dress.

Demious said we could wander during the day, but there was never enough time. I had wanted to explore the maze since arriving and now seemed like the perfect time. If I didn't focus on something other than what that man just did to me, I would scream so loud, every creature in Farrow's Gate would run away.

The entrance started underneath an iron gate with wild vines. The trimmed hedges were about eleven feet high. I turned inside, gripping my dress. Though most of the maze held nothing but bush, a turn here led to a secret sculpture of an animal, another turn brought me to a door leading nowhere, another held a bunch of wild roses, the perfect spot for a secret kiss.

But after the tenth or thirteenth turn, I panicked.

The maze didn't seem that large outside. Why couldn't I find an exit or the center?

The next pathway led to a fork. I turned right.

Dead end.

I swiveled around and retraced my steps, but I hadn't paid attention to where I'd walked.

"Baine?" I called out, knowing he had to be close.

Did he follow me in here? I can't take any more surprises tonight.

Night stars replaced the pink and purple sky. Clouds rolled in covering the moon. How long had I been out here? A breeze rustled the leaves on the bushes.

"Baine?" This time I whispered his name, suddenly afraid he hadn't followed me inside this tricky labyrinth, and I was lost. "Please, tell me you're here."

Something *swooshed* by me, sending my dress twirling. I turned but saw nothing.

My heart raced. I had to get out of here.

"Baine!"

"I'm here."

I jumped at the sound of his voice by my ear. "Don't scare me!"

He narrowed his gaze and that smoldering look set my already heightened body on fire. "I thought you might like to walk alone."

We were a foot apart, me glancing up into those light eyes.

He didn't need to say anything, the pity was written all over his face.

Baine was close to Lord Demious and with a little nudging, he might tell me what I needed to know about this competition and the collar. Staying wasn't an option, especially after Lord Demious' little display. No matter how much I wanted to clear my debt, I would not bind my life to that vileness. I'd find another way. I had to.

With a furrowed brow, Baine reached over and took my arm. His thumb rubbed over the area where Lord Demious had grabbed me, the skin red.

"Is he always like that?" I asked, trying hard not to let my emotions roll out in a bumbling mess.

"Depends on the situation." Baine brushed his fingers across my skin. "I can bring you back and have your servant tend to it."

"That's all right. I'm fine. Will you escort me to the center of the maze?" I held out my arm for him to take like a proper gentleman. "Please, I don't want to go back inside."

When he glared at me, I thought he would send me away, instead, he surprised me by slipping his arm around mine.

His closeness caused my heart to run wild and my mind to think of dangerous thoughts—a stark difference from the clammy touch of Lord Demious. Afraid of scaring the fae off, I kept quiet as he led us through the maze to the middle where we were rewarded with a massive three-tiered fountain. A fae woman with raised arms stood in the center of the fountain. She held a silver disc with sparkling gems.

"I need to see this closer."

"That's a bad idea," Baine said, one step behind me.

"Stop worrying and give me your hand."

He held out his hand, and I used it to steady myself and get a foothold. Once I was secure, I stepped onto the ledge of the square fountain.

"It's beautiful." The elven face had been carved out of sparkling white marble, and every curve, detailed and perfect.

I stood on my tip toes, glancing at the red gems.

"Miss Hawk."

"Rosalie," I corrected. "Call me Rosalie or Rose."

His brow knitted together. "Fine, Rosalie. It's time to return."

He held out his hand and I shooed him away. "I can get down by myself. I don't need—"

My words caught in my throat as my dress caught under my foot, sending me tumbling forward. Thankfully, my dark guardian had better balance than I did and caught me in his arms.

If there were ever a time to be graceful, I wish this had been it.

Instead of a romantic rescue, I gripped his neck while half of my dress smothered his face and one leg awkwardly hung around one of his arms.

"Well, that's embarrassing," I mumbled and slowly tried to right myself.

Baine growled, I'm pretty sure from annoyance, and flipped me around until he was carrying me and my puffy dress like a baby. My arms slipped lower and as my fingers grazed his neck, the scowl on his face shifted to something else.

Fae, dwarf, human, no matter what the race, all males held the same hungry stare when a female did something they liked: that hooded gaze, the tightness in their jaw, the way their neck tilted in the slightest direction.

I don't know what possessed me, but without asking permission, I reached up and touched the piece of silver hair that curled right by his ear. When he didn't hiss, or scowl, I gently dragged my finger along the edge of his earlobe, examining how slender and long his ear was compared to mine. Fae were as mythical as the stories I had heard growing up. They tended to keep to their woods and cities, and shifting fae? I never dreamed I'd get to meet one. I reached up and touched the very tip of Baine's ear. He shuddered and a low growl left his pink lips.

"What are you doing?" he said gruffly.

"Are fae ears very sensitive?"

"Yes."

Running my fingers along the point of his ear, I asked, "How sensitive are they?"

His jaw twitched. "You shouldn't do that."

Laughter trickled in from somewhere in the maze. Baine's expression turned to stone, and he swiftly dashed into another part of the garden. The quick movement made my head spin, and I blinked back the wave of vertigo hitting me.

When he set me on my feet, we were in another hidden area. A dangerous glint festered in his light eyes. I kept his intense gaze, uncertainty running through every inch of me as he pressed me against the ivy-covered wall. Sweet wine lingered on his breath.

Without a word, Baine took my arm and dragged his finger lazily across my bare forearm. The slow stroke sent a ripple of energy coursing through my body. The flame inside sparked to life, a tiny flicker, still dampened by the magic, but there. A simple gesture, yet for some reason my senses came alive. I needed more and tugged Baine closer, desperate to ignite the spark buried inside me. Those rough fingers of his danced on my skin, little bolts of warmth lighting me up. When he lifted his gaze to mine, there was a softness there, and curiosity?

Baine abruptly stepped back. "Your eyes."

I heaved with wild emotions. Strange, wild feelings that confused and excited me, nothing like the stolen kisses and touches from when I played with the baker's son near our family's barn.

This was different, *very* different.

"Rosalie."

More laughter sounded from the other side of the wall. Baine lifted me off the ground and ran. The wind rushed my skin, cooling me. I didn't know how far or long he ran, but when he finally stopped, we were on the other side of the estate, and the heat inside me had extinguished.

"What happened back there?" He laid me on the grass and crouched in front of me.

My belly warmed at the memory of his touch. "Do you want me to repeat it, or shall we continue?"

He scowled, and I pouted. *Great, we're back to that.*

"Your eyes turned to flames."

"My what?"

"Your eyes. They switched from blue to fire and your skin heated."

A twinge of panic set in. I knew his touch had awakened my magic, but I didn't understand why, or how, or what Baine thought of it. Did it mean I could possibly break through the dampening power of the choker I wore? Could I be that powerful? What would happen to my flame if Baine and I kissed?

I played with the hem of my dress. "Oh, I

don't know."

The slight idea of Baine's touch awakening my power sent my mind whirling with possibilities.

Baine grabbed my chin and forced me to look at him. "You do."

No matter how much Baine excited me, he couldn't know the truth. Not with my brother at the Borderlands. If word of my elemental heritage spread, they would throw him to the frontlines, and I would lose him forever. Nothing was worth that risk. Plus, I had a feeling if Lord Demious knew I was half elemental, I'd be the unfortunate winner of his competition.

When I didn't answer, Baine released me. "We need to return. It's been too long."

He took my hand and helped me stand, but quickly let go.

"Yes," I said, turning away from him. "I wouldn't want anyone to miss me."

I didn't wait for Baine to respond or to follow. I stormed off toward the estate, desperate to make sense of this revelation and how I could use it to my advantage.

SEVEN

BAINE

Activating my ability, I dashed in front of Rosalie.

"Wait." I held out my hands, stopping her.

The quick movement caused her to gasp. "Stop doing that."

"We must return from the gardens," I said, glancing at our surroundings. I'd taken her to the opposite side of the estate, far from the party. "Otherwise, there may be questions."

A rose hue tainted her pale cheeks. "Why? Did we do something wrong?"

"I . . ." For once, I had no answer. Thinking back, we did nothing wrong, yet I knew my actions had been too forward. The wine had dulled my logic, and I acted like a fool. "No, but it's not proper for you and me to be alone like this."

Without thinking, I swept her into my arms.

Once I carried us swiftly back into the gardens, far enough from the party, I set her down.

She groaned and grabbed her head. "I really hate it when you do that."

Placing a hand on her back to steady her, I noticed her body still ran hot. Was that her magic? "Close your eyes and the queasiness will disappear."

Another groan.

Taking her hand, I led her to a bench and sat next to her.

"Thank you," she said with a sigh. "It's been an awfully long few days, and I miss my home. This is all so . . ."

"Unexpected?"

She smiled. "Yes, very. If I had known the troll planned on selling me to be a bride, I would've found another way to save my home."

"Where is your family?" We knew little about her past, anything I could learn would be useful.

"My parents died a year ago. My twin left for war, and it's just been me." She gazed up at the stars. One of the white monarch moths flew overhead. Its wings had a smearing of okra and red hues. "I need to go home."

A moment of silence stretched between us, and I allowed her to have it. While I had been around human females before, this one seemed different, nothing like the nobles Lord Demious entertained. No one had dared to ever speak to the magistrate the way she did. Yet, she showed courage when it came to her home. This human was more than what she seemed.

"Rosalie, we need to discuss what happened in the maze."

Her cheeks reddened. "Which parts?"

"The part when your eyes turned to fire."

Her brow furrowed, but she didn't answer.

I tried asking a bit softer. "The magical energy in Farrow's Gate is different from the rest of Saol. If there's any danger—"

"I'm not a danger." She turned to me, her expression falling somewhere between hopelessness and fear. "I swear I only want to return home. I have no ill will here."

"I cannot help you, if you're not honest with me."

"Will you?"

I arched a brow at her.

She took my hand and clenched it tightly. "Will you help me?"

"I give you my word, what is spoken between us tonight will not leave this maze." Beyond my better judgment, I stroked the side of her cheek. "Your words are safe with me. Tell me. How did your magic break through the dampener?"

Her face flushed, and she glanced away from me. "If you don't know, then you're not the fae I thought you were."

Uneasiness coursed through me at the way she peeked at me beneath those thick lashes, making me question why I was still out here with her. How could her magic bypass the dampener around her neck? And what did that mean?

"Baine," she said, while watching the moths dance in the twilight. "Can I ask you something?"

"Yes," I replied, much too quickly.

The moonlight cast directly into her blue eyes, highlighting the sprinkles of green I hadn't noticed before. A unique and beautiful color.

"Do you think Lord Demious will help my hawks? I can't abandon them, and they'll die if I don't do something soon."

I thought for a moment. After his display, I knew he would not let her leave the estate, but he was not unreasonable when it came to magical affairs. "If you were to marry, you would have the power to help them yourself."

She scrunched up the front of her dress within her hands. "And will he be a kind husband or choke me with his black death when I don't submit to his wills?"

Realizing what she asked, I answered honestly. "Lord Demious may be eccentric, but he will treat his wife well. He did not lie when he said his wife would be his equal. The magistrate is many things, but he will stay true to his word."

"That's good to know." Rosalie stood and smoothed out her dress, her bottom lip trembling. "I'm ready to return now."

Her expression and tone had a frankness to it. She'd resigned herself to this bride competition and to the idea of being Lord Demious' wife.

And that bothered me.

Eight

Rosalie

If there was one thing I learned from the few days being at Farrow's Gate, it was that anyone who ended up marrying Lord Demious would be bored for the rest of their life. He sat at the head of the table, cutting his buttery biscuit into tiny pieces, and dipping each of those tiny, so tiny, pieces into the bowl of soup.

"I have something special today, my ladies," he said, dotting the napkin to his mouth. "We are leaving the estate."

Murmurs spread around the breakfast table, and I dropped my roll into the soup bowl with a plop.

"Before there are any ideas of escape, know

that while the spell to leave the barrier around my home will be temporarily disabled, the collars will continue to negate your magic. Our guards will make sure no one gets any ideas of leaving."

I'd expect nothing less. Not like I would run away, at least not yet. My problems would still be there when I got home, and I would be right back where I was before I sold myself off. After last night, I had a terrible sinking feeling that if I got caught escaping those black claws of his would crawl into my mouth and choke me from the inside. Unlike the rest of the girls here, I didn't have anyone back home who would be searching for me if I suddenly disappeared. I didn't even know if Calvin was still alive.

Glancing around at the chattering girls, each seemed excited about today's walk about the town, if that's where we were even going. How could they be excited? Did these girls actually want to marry him? How could they? Okay, so he wasn't terrible to look at, handsome even, but between his droning on about himself and the creepy shadow magic, how could any sensible person want to marry him?

"Have you ever been to town?" Janetta whispered.

"Only when I came here, but I think I slept

through that part." I recoiled in disgust at the memory of those two weeks spent in that urine drenched wagon.

"I've always wanted to see it. My mother said the entire town is a shimmering color of blues and oranges."

I realized I knew nothing about Janetta. Not where she came from, or why she was here. "Where's your home?"

She smiled, gazing out at the open window, almost like she was visualizing the place. "Imagine a cozy village with wide arching trees covered in the greenest moss and stone cobbled roads that wind around thatched cottages each decorated with flowers and plants. Wildflowers, birds that sing day and night, and babbling brooks connecting all of it together."

"Sounds beautiful."

"It is." She turned to me and grabbed my hand. "Promise me, that one day you will come to Aoife and meet my family."

I squeezed her hand, accepting the offer even though I knew Janetta and I would probably never see each other again after this "competition."

"Of course," I promised.

Satisfied, she let go of me and picked up her spoon to finish her soup. "What about you? Where's your home?"

A servant stepped in between us. "Tea?"

"Yes, please." I waited until the servant had poured the drink before answering.

A sweet, rich scent wafted off the hot liquid. I picked up one of the smaller spoons, which I assumed was for tea, and stirred the liquid around, carefully blowing on it. "I don't come from anywhere special. Just a wild girl from the North. We've got woods, wildcats, and too many briar bushes."

Janetta laughed, causing Lord Demious to arch a brow in our direction. She covered her mouth, and we spent the next few minutes finishing our meals in silence.

At the end of the meal, Ms. Begalia clapped her hands. "Attention girls, attention! We will be leaving the dining hall, exiting the main entrance, and heading outside where the carriages await."

Inwardly groaning, I gazed around at all the other prospects.

Out of the ten girls present, I was a hag compared to some. If I was old enough to handle a bunch of firehawks on my own, I didn't need some old mistress bossing me around. I was too old for this nonsense.

While Ms. Begalia herded us outside like a bunch of cattle, I thought back to my conversation with Baine. For a brief moment, I imagined what being married to Lord Demious would be like . . . the thought of his face close to mine made my stomach curl and I instantly dismissed the idea.

No, not an option.

Even if Baine did mention Lord Demious was a kind man, I couldn't trust him. Not after he chided me with his magic in the gardens.

"Girls," Ms. Begalia's high-pitched voice grated on my ears. "Into the carriage. You two go in that one."

Janetta stepped into the black carriage waiting outside the mansion. One more carriage parked behind it with guards mounted on horses flanking both.

Baine rode a black horse, dressed in all black leathers. The silver hilts of his twin swords sparkled under the afternoon sun. Our gazes met, his mouth drawn in a firm line, showing no emotion, or any hint of the fae I had entertained last night.

Something poked my back and I turned around to Ms. Begalia prodding me with the tip of her parasol. Keeping my comments to myself, I ignored her and her mole and climbed inside after Janetta.

Of course, Ms. Begalia would put me in the same carriage as the three sisters.

The younger one smiled. "Hi, we haven't met,

I'm Chloe."

"Hi," I said to the smiling girl. She may have looked exactly like her brunette older sisters, but without the glaring and frowning.

"Have you been to the town?" Chloe tapped her feet against the floor. "It's unlike any other places in Saol. Well, maybe not all. I hear the fairy village in the Nightsong Jungle is the most magical place."

It bothered me that this young, sweet girl was being subjected to a competition, and against her sisters. She couldn't be more than sixteen. "I haven't. Janetta said it was lovely."

"Enough, Chloe. Don't bother with the rabble." Claudia folded her arms across her navy dress. The servants must've tightened her corset extra tight today with the way she sat and glared.

Chloe pouted. Apparently, she didn't share her sister's sentiments. Maybe I should've made a quick remark back, but what was the point? If they wanted to be mean, let them.

Ignoring my temporary carriage mates, I leaned against the side of the carriage, peeking outside at the passing landscape. Farrow's Gate had an ethereal beauty. The grass shifted colors with the wind, rolling from cerulean to cobalt to teal. There was nothing else like it, and as I rested my arm on the edge of the open window and inhaled the peony scented breeze, I thought back to a simpler time. Back to when my father would throw fireballs at me and my brother. Back to when my mother would play the violin and dance around the fire in her bare feet, kicking up dust and laughter. Back to when my family was alive and together.

Work kept me going after they passed. What happened to them was no one's fault, which meant I had nowhere to send my anger. Work became therapeutic. When I wanted to cry, I picked up a shovel. When I couldn't sleep, I weeded our gardens until my fingers bled and my shoulders were sun-kissed.

Home. I *needed* to get back home.

Hooves sounded outside, and I stuck my head out the window to see which of the guards was riding by. Baine galloped past me like a shadow disappearing in the sunlight, right to the front of our little train. Using my hand to shield the sunlight from my eyes, I tried to see who he was talking to. As if sensing me lurking in the distance, he glanced back over his shoulder, and I quickly slid back into my seat.

"Look." Janetta patted my arm and pointed outside. "Do you see it?"

Towering steep rock walls stretched for miles across cerulean grass and vivid green. A roaring sound echoed off everything coming from water rushing from the top of the cliffs and descending below. Above the soaring cliffs, a kaleidoscope of colors shimmered in the sky, pale pinks, and iridescent purples. Nestled in the valley beneath the cliffs sat a town with starch white houses, gray-steepled buildings, and majestic eagles that glided across the pastures stocked full of fat brown cattle and wild horses.

"This is the heart of Farrow's Gate?" The stories could never describe the awe-inspiring view. I didn't think anything could relate to the sight before me.

"Isn't it pretty?" Chloe chimed in. "I hope Lord Demious takes us to the tower. That's one of my favorite spots."

Why would Lord Demious dangle this treasure in front of us? To toy with our feelings? Force us to show off our abilities to become a lady of this place? I had a duty to my home, and my animals, and I wouldn't be swayed with pretty landscapes.

Though, if I was being honest, it was more than pretty.

Our caravan followed the road into the bottom of the valley and through the town. Sabers, the beast race of Saol, walked freely amongst humans, wearing skins, and carrying long spears, but that wasn't the end of the diverse population. Farrow's Gate had a hodgepodge of races: dwarfs, gnomes, even the fair skinned fae of Criostail with their glittering white hair and luminescent eyes. So many different races, all of them mingling and busying about the day in perfect harmony.

It seemed silly, but part of me wondered if Farrow's Gate would welcome a half-breed like me. A place where my brother and I could start new. And the firehawks? They would love this valley, but leaving the North wasn't an option with those blasted plague snakes infecting everything. If I could find someone to remove the snakes completely, maybe one day we could move somewhere else. We'd come close to eradicating the invasive species until the hawks became sick.

The carriages stopped in front of a slate-gray tower with three steeples and an ominous sculpture of a beast perched on the highest point.

Ms. Begalia's crude voice ruined the beauty of the afternoon with her orders and demands, forcing us all into perfect lines. Lord Demious stood next to Baine, watching us, outfitted in a nutmeg-colored suit and brocade vest. It did nothing for his appearance, and I wondered if Ms. Begalia oversaw his clothing.

"This here is the host tower," she said, waving

her hand at the building in front of us. "All throughout Saol, these towers exist to study the magic within the land and make sure everything is balanced. As the future lady of Farrow's Gate, you will be expected to assist the tower in any disturbances within the valley."

Whispers and confused glances exchanged amongst the girls.

Lord Demious held up a hand. "I know it seems strange to bestow such a heavy burden on my future wife, but it is necessary." He clasped his hands behind his back, smiling at us as he walked back and forth.

"You see, in Farrow's Gate, a marriage is one of power. My bride must be strong enough to deal with the tower and assist the people of my city."

"What do you do?" Chloe asked, causing Claudia to pinch her side and scowl at the younger girl.

Lord Demious brushed off the interruption and laughed. "An honest question. Do you see the sky?"

We all looked up.

"One day at sunset during the moon cycle, I must meditate and renew the barriers that keep the wild magic contained within our land. While I do handle political discussions and larger problems, my wife must be able to stand on her own. Without both of us doing our part, our barrier will weaken, and the wild magic will seep out into the surrounding area."

"And before you ask why that is bad," he paused, smirking at Chloe who stared at him with wide eyes, "the wild magic transforms and can change a simple rabbit into something dangerous. Life is a balance and within this system at Farrow's Gate, we've established that. Now, enough talk, into the tower where you will see for yourself."

A massive door opened, scraping along the cobbled road. My heart did a strange pitter-patter. I shouldn't be nervous. I had no reason to be. So why did stepping into the tower send an odd chill down my spine?

One by one we followed Lord Demious inside the building with Baine and a human guard taking up the rear, the remaining force staying behind. The area around my collar itched, and I dug my fingers into the space between the metal and my neck. Scratching at my sweaty skin, I searched the area for anything that might shout a warning about walking into this tower.

The ground floor held nothing but stone, a massive hall with closed doors, and a spiraling staircase that wound up and out of view. Something tugged on my dress, and I turned to Alicia, who gaped at the stairs in horror.

"It's okay. I'm sure it's safe." One flimsy wooden railing that seemed out of place in all the stone surely could hold us, right?

With a gentle nudge, I guided Alicia in front of me and behind Janetta. The quiet girl barely spoke and when she did, the sentences were few. Not only could I not picture her marrying that snore of a lord, but working as a slave for him? How did someone as frail and gentle as this girl end up here?

Surprisingly, Ms. Begalia's nagging had diminished to soft-spoken assurances that the stairs would hold, that we were fine, and Lord Demious would never put his lovely prospects in harm's way.

Placing my hand on the rough wood, I took the winding stone steps one at a time and braced myself for the worst.

NINE

BAINE

Lord Demious had explained that morning his idea to bring the prospects to the crone. Every tower had a mage, but only one had a crone. Crones were a particular odd race in Saol. At one point they had been human, then the magic twisted their bodies, turning them into creatures who walked and talked like a human, yet resembled the raptors who flew in our skies.

Crones held a deep affinity for magic, scenting it like they would a flower, able to determine the type from a single drop of blood. Lord Demious was taking this bridal competition way too seriously, even for him.

The group stopped on the third floor before continuing to the top to the crone's laboratory.

"Ms. Begalia," Lord Demious called out over the talking females huddled together. "Take the girls into the library while I make sure our host is ready to meet us."

I nodded at the young human guard I brought in, Aster, to go in first and do a quick sweep. He waded through the throng of females until he disappeared inside the room.

Rosalie spoke with another girl, whispering quickly. She bunched the sides of her dress in her hands. Was she nervous? Did she know about the crone? If my tattoo allowed me to sense her magic, the crone would identify the magnitude of it.

The servants had braided Rosalie's long hair into twists on the top of her head. The style displayed the soft curve of her neck and the open back of her dress. Most of the girls dressed in similar attire, with the Haalow females seeming to show off any asset they could, but none of them had the womanly curves like Rosalie, and not just curves. Hands rough from working, toned arms reflecting hours spent toiling the land, and a hardiness that could only be earned by spending years in the wilds.

Aster whistled from the open doorway and nodded that we were clear.

"Everyone inside," I said, walking forward.

The group's chattering increased, and the females eagerly went into the massive library, except Rosalie. Her eyes widened as I approached.

"What is it?" She had no cause to look so terrified, yet she did.

Once her friend had ventured into the library, Rosalie shuffled closer until only I could hear her speak. "Why are we here? What is he going to do with us?"

"Nothing. Why are you rattled?"

She gripped the front of her dress, gaze flitting all around the area, almost searching for a hidden threat. "It doesn't feel right. There's something wrong about this place. Don't you feel it?"

For a moment, I closed off my mind and used my fae senses to listen, to scent, and find the cause of her unsettled behavior. I had been to this tower many times, and the only thing odd about it was the host who lived here.

Taking Rosalie's elbow, I turned her toward the library. "Nothing will harm you here. Go with the others."

"But . . ."

Realizing she would need a little more persuasion, I placed a hand on her back and walked with her. "You need not worry here.

Lord Demious would not have brought any of you to the tower if he thought you'd be in danger. I wasn't lying when I said he protects his people, and right now all of you are under his protection."

The tips of my fingers touched her soft skin where the dress tied together. The connection sent a spark through me, and I didn't know if I wanted to remove my hand or keep it there. Regardless of my desires, Rosalie calmed at my touch and entered the library. Only after she stepped over the threshold, did I remove myself and take guard by the door.

Instead of joining the others while they gawked at the rows of ancient texts, Rosalie drifted deeper into the library and out of my sight. I motioned for Aster to take position by the entrance, and I followed her.

The library resided in the larger steeple of the tower. Ceilings high enough to accompany birds and long narrow windows brought enough sunlight to not need any type of lantern or candle inside. Iron railings surrounded the second and third floor of the library, accompanied by paintings so old dust cluttered the images. If this had been any other tower, the host mage would have had servants cleaning every sacred place. The crones worked and lived alone for hundreds of years. They desired only quiet and darkness, and the company of others like them.

They had only one desire: magic.

Some of the more ancient crones lived off consuming rare magics. The only item they seemed to crave were life crystals, the golden gems of the All Father scattered across Saol to protect itself and its citizens from darkness.

Crones hated anything that put those gems at risk, more than they hated anything else, which was why they made excellent allies against the darkthings. The life crystals were not only used in objects to combat darkthings, but they healed any wound from the creature. As darkness continued to creep into the land from the Rift in the Never, the amount of life crystals diminished. No one, not even the magi, could replicate the mineral and the crystals seemed to take decades to regrow on their own—and Saol was running out of time.

Examining the area, I noticed Rosalie had wandered away from her friends. She trailed her fingers along the rows of books, staring at them with a keen interest. A brass spiral staircase led to the second floor, and without hesitation, she climbed up the stairs.

What is she doing?

From my vantage point, I could still see her until she went down a row and the iron railing obscured my view, forcing me to chase after the precarious human.

When I hit the second floor, I headed toward the last place I saw her.

Empty.

Walking down another aisle, I peeked around the rows of books.

Empty.

I stopped, listening to the sounds around me and ignoring the talking below. Scurries of a mouse, a rustling of curtains from one of the nearby windows, but no breaths, no footsteps.

Rosalie had simply vanished.

TEN

ROSALIE

The moment my hand pressed the stone statue, I knew I'd made a mistake. The secret passageway swung around, locking me in on the other side into a dimly lit corridor. Spiderwebs hung from the ceilings and around the lanterns sporadically placed in the narrow hall. Quickly, I searched the closed wall for a latch or anything that might get me out of this place and back into the library.

"Hello?" I banged on the wall, hoping someone would hear me. "Hello? Anyone? Hello!"

When no one came to my rescue, I decided the only thing to do was to move forward into the extremely creepy passageway and hope it led to an exit.

I sneezed and covered my mouth. Not only did this place have a century of dust but something must've died within the walls, leaving a horrid scent that made my throat burn. If I had a knife on me, I would've sliced my dress and made a face covering. Instead, I wore another ridiculous outfit that's only function was to show off my breasts.

Covering my nose and mouth slightly, I walked, heading in the only direction available, searching the stone-lined walls for anything resembling an exit.

The passageway turned up, spiraling just like the stairs outside the library. Keeping one hand to the wall, I stepped slowly, keeping my gaze ahead.

Something scurried behind me, and I squeaked at the rat running up the stairs.

I bet he knows where to go.

Following the rodent, I chased the creature up the staircase until it ended at a black door. Light beamed from under the doorway and the rat slid between the space, leaving me alone. Before going in, I pressed my ear against the wood and listened, and when I heard nothing but my own heartbeat, I opened the door.

I don't know what I expected, but it wasn't

an empty room, or at least empty of anything exciting. The door shut behind me and I jumped.

"I need to get out of this place."

Half of the room hid in darkness, obscuring anything interesting. The side I entered was on the south of the room, and since the entire left portion of the room hid within a blanket of shadow, I moved toward the right near a swaying red curtain leading to a balcony.

Pieces of straw scattered across the stone floor. There were no paintings, no decorations, not even a chair for someone to sit, and why was there straw? An odd musty scent reminding me of moldy hay filled the room, making my eyes water.

Focusing on the sunlight creeping in from the swaying curtain, I stepped slowly, crunching straw as I walked. Coldness crept up my back, and I swung around, staring at the shadows. My heart raced.

"Hello?"

When no one responded, I turned and moved toward the balcony.

A strong breeze blew inside the room, kicking up the surrounding straw.

Growing up in the woods, I learned a lot about beasts and the fear that came when you knew the wildcat stalked you through the forest.

That horrid sense of dread filled me now,

making my hands and arms shake. My flame flickered as if it knew I was in danger but was snuffed out by the magic wrapped around my throat.

I didn't want to turn around.

I *knew* something was there.

But if I had learned anything from my father, it was that we didn't run from our fear, we embraced it, and met the danger head on with courage. With a steadying breath, fists raised, I slowly turned around.

Two glowing eyes watched me from the shadows. From this distance, I knew whatever lurked on the other side of the room was twice my size, at least.

"Whooo goess in my towerrrr?"

The deep, scratching voice made me step back. "No one. I'm lost."

The creature stepped forward just enough to let the light shine on its massive form, hidden beneath tattered black robes. "Youuu tresspasss."

"No, I meant no offense." Holding my hands up in a silent plea, I searched for an escape. There had to be another exit out of this room.

The creature stalked forward, and quicker than I expected, snatched my arm, and lifted me off the ground. Clawed fingers dug into my skin as it dangled me in front of it. The hood fell away as the thing sniffed me and I screamed.

Withered, wrinkled skin, surrounded a black curled beak and beady yellow eyes. Black feathers covered the sinewy arm that held me, but not the head. The creature's bald head reminded me of the vultures that ate the dead things near the mountain pass in the North. Those were tiny compared to the thing that held me. This thing had to be at least eight feet tall.

It brought me to its nose where it dragged its bony beak across my neck. "Magiccccc."

I twisted in its grasp. "Let me go!"

With its other hand, it swiped a claw across my forehead, ripping the skin open. I screamed at the pain and kicked the creature in the stomach.

Unphased by my attempts to attack, it held me out of reach with one arm and put the bloody claw in its mouth. Its eyes glowed bright, almost golden, and it hissed.

"Eleeemeentaallll." The way it groaned out the word made my fight or flight instincts kick in. "Youuu will diiieee herrreee."

It bit into my forearm and began drinking my blood. Screaming, I swung my legs back and forth, kicking as hard as I could and using my body as a pendulum. The creature sucked on my skin, a strange tingling running through my body, making my head dizzy. Blood slid down my arm and I swung my legs, desperately trying to dislodge myself.

Nausea filled my body, and I knew that if this thing drank anymore, whatever poison it infected me with would kill me. Suddenly, it screeched and dropped me, hissing at my blood, and shaking its head.

"You taste like firreeeee."

I landed hard on the stone, scrambled to my feet and sprinted toward the open balcony. The creature roared and trampled over to me. I gripped the leg of the stone banister of the balcony just as the creature grabbed my legs.

"No!" I kicked at the claws ripping my skin.

The robes had fallen and standing over me was some mix of human-bird creature, twice my size and more powerful than anything I'd ever encountered. Massive black wings unfurled from its back as it stood to its full height.

All Father protect me.

"Rosalie!" I heard Baine's voice call from outside.

The yell distracted the creature for a moment, and I kicked myself free from its grasp. I pulled myself up and leaned over the balcony. Baine stood on the ground outside.

"Here! I'm here! There's something—"

My words were cut off as claws wrapped around my neck, squeezing me. "Youuuu will not escapppeee. I willlll feeed."

Baine's face twisted in shock and fear. He was too far from me and not even his speed could reach me now.

The creature lifted me off the ground, holding me by my neck. My flame flickered, desperate to escape, but even the slight heat emanating from my body did nothing to stop the thing clutching me.

"You will do no such thing." Lord Demious' voice sounded behind me.

Relief filled me.

I was saved.

I smiled at Baine, knowing I would be okay.

And then the creature let me go.

Right over the balcony.

ELEVEN

BAINE

"No!" I screamed as Rosalie fell from the sky, fear and panic haunting her blue eyes.

A spark of magic zapped from the balcony, encasing her in a shimmering bubble, slowing her descent. I ran and held out my arms until she fell into them.

"Get the prospects out of that tower!" I screamed at my men, knowing Lord Demious would need to subdue the crone before the creature went into a frenzy.

Blood spewed from a bite on Rosalie's arm and dripped from a gash in her forehead. Gripping her tightly, I moved away from the tower to a safer distance. I needed to stop the bleeding.

"What is that thing?" Her body shook in my arms.

"A crone, this tower's host mage."

"That . . . that's who Lord Demious brought us to meet?" Her shaking intensified, making her teeth chatter against one another.

"You entered its nest. One of the few things that will provoke the creature. They are very territorial."

"I . . . I didn't know." Her body trembled.

I couldn't wait. I had to take her somewhere.

But that meant leaving Lord Demious alone to deal with the crone. Though, he could handle the beast, I didn't like the idea of leaving him.

"Baine." Rosalie buried her face within the folds of my shirt, gripping the material in her hands. "I . . . I don't feel so good."

Holding her close, I touched her face. Her normally warm skin was ice cold. "Hold on."

The fast movement would make her queasy, but I had no choice. She needed a healer, and quickly.

With her cradled in my arms, I flew across the grass, running toward the healer's cottage by the Moonlake waterfall, less than a mile from our current position. Rosalie's hold on me slipped, her hands releasing my shirt as she lost consciousness.

Once Lord Demious saw I was gone, he would know where I went and send word. For now, I had one objective, make sure this fragile human in my arms didn't die.

The healer hated uninvited visits. I'd need to pay her well.

"Enola!" I screamed, banging on the door of the cottage with my fist.

Her goat ate at the grass by the side of the house. She never left home without him.

"Enola!" Banging again, I yelled for the healer to come forth. If she didn't answer, I'd kick in the door and find the herbs I needed.

The door swung inward, and I stepped back.

"What in all of Saol is the matter! I'm trying to nap." Her angry glare softened when she noticed Rosalie. "Who is that?"

"She needs help."

"Bring her in." Enola closed the door behind me. "To the bed."

Gently, I laid Rosalie down. The sunlight from the window near the bed highlighted the sickly paleness of her skin. I kneeled on the ground beside her head, brushing her hair off her face.

Enola pulled over a wooden chair and sat. "What happened?" She picked up Rosalie's arm, examining the circular wound.

"The crone."

"The crone? He hasn't attacked anyone in decades." Enola went to her workbench where herbs dangled from hooks and hung in bunches. "I'll need more yarrow. For now, I'll dress the wound and put on the kettle. Some stinging nettle tea will help fight any infection."

"Baine." Enola eyed me as she returned with a bunch of cotton. "This wound. You know what it is and what it means?"

My instincts told me what I didn't want to believe.

"If the crone tried to eat her, her magic is at high levels. They won't devour anything mundane." Enola swabbed the wound before wrapping the cotton around Rosalie's arm. "We've known each other a long time."

"We have." Lord Demious introduced me to Enola when she was a young maid. Now the skin around her eyes crinkled when she smiled, she walked a tad slower, and her dark hair had streaks of gray. Yet, her gaze held a vibrance and vitality that rivaled the elven queens.

"Who is she? Why was she near the crone?"

There was no worry of Enola running off and gossiping. Those trivial things were beneath the woman. "She is one of Lord Demious' bride prospects."

Enola scoffed. "I had heard of that ridiculous competition. The man is getting more eccentric in his old age. He thought to have the crone test their blood, didn't he?"

"He's determined to have the most powerful bride. He believes Farrow's Gate won't survive unless his lineage is secured with another powerful mage."

"If the man wasn't so loyal to his subjects, I'd bop him on the head for his stupidity."

I smiled. Enola may have been the only human alive who could do that and live.

She stood. "I need to go get more yarrow. Let the nettle sit for a few minutes before you make the girl drink it."

Enola grabbed a wicker basket off the table and left.

After today's events, there was no questioning that Rosalie hid her true potential. Even Lord Demious would question the attack unless he didn't find out. In all my years of service, I had never betrayed the magistrate. I'd been loyal, both as the head of his guard and as his friend. If I told Lord Demious the crone attempted to drink Rosalie's blood, it would seal his decision to marry her.

Could I lie for her?

Would I?

Marrying Lord Demious would resolve her debt and her farm would be her own again, but that also meant I would spend the rest of my life watching the two of them together, and that bothered me. There was also the matter of her firehawks. After Lord Demious' odd display in the maze, I questioned whether he would care about her request. Lately, he seemed more on edge than usual. What would Rosalie do if she did marry the lord and he refused to save her flock?

Needing to clear my thoughts, I went to make the tea. Taking the iron kettle off the stone oven, I poured the steaming liquid into the mug with the nettle leaves.

Why did this female make me question my allegiance? Why was I even here? If it had been any other prospect, I would have handed her over to another guard and ran into the tower, swords drawn, eager to fight by Lord Demious' side.

What are you doing to me, human?

A silent question that would go unanswered.

Soft breaths left her lips as she slept. The more time I spent in her company, the more intrigued I became. Most women would be honored for a chance to become a lady, but not Rosalie. She wanted her farm and nothing else.

If only my own family had been as loyal to me.

Taking a spoon, I stirred the tea.

Once I had been like Rosalie, protecting those

I loved no matter the cost. That dedication had me exiled from my own home. There were rules in Saol, some unspoken, some known to all. I had broken the most important rule among my people: no prisoners of war. Being a young fae, I knew that rule, believed in it, until the day my people tried to slaughter a coven of human children we had once cared for. These children were from a nearby village, one I had visited often to exchange goods. Sweet, innocent little ones who only wanted to play with the little ball I always brought and tell me jokes.

Then the fae went to war with those humans, and the whole village was to be destroyed, including the children. I couldn't allow such slaughter, and I did what my people forbade. Under the cover of night, using my swiftness ability, I took every single child I could find and brought them to safety.

And how did the humans repay me for that kindness? By capturing me like a wild beast when I was sleeping, exhausted from saving their kin. If Lord Demious hadn't happened to come across the human encampment during his travels and rescue me, I'd be dead.

Balling my fists, I looked at the human sleeping on the bed. She was nothing like those humans. She reminded me of my younger self, stubborn, foolish, and protective of things that were dear to her.

"Rosalie," I said softly as I sat in the chair next to the bed.

When she didn't respond, I moved to the bed and slid her over, positioning myself behind her body. Carefully, I held the tea in one hand and used my other arm to lift Rosalie into my lap until her back rested against my chest. "You must drink this."

Again, she continued to sleep. Using one hand, I tilted her head back and opened her mouth with a finger. I blew on the mug a few times before bringing it to her lips and very slowly poured the drink into her mouth. She stirred, drinking the liquid, though her eyes remained closed. When she finished the tea, she turned into me, nuzzling against my shirt.

I placed the empty mug on the windowsill by the bed and wrapped both arms around the sleeping human. I gazed out at the large windows facing Moonlake. The waterfall plunged into the serene pool, misting the area and the large pink lotus flowers that decorated the shores.

Rosalie warmed within my grasp, her temperature returning to normal. I sighed in relief, knowing her innate magic would help the healing process.

The door to the cottage opened and I tensed,

realizing in this position I couldn't reach my swords. Enola stepped in carrying a basket of tiny yellow flowers. Her gaze flitted to Rosalie then to me.

I froze. I knew how this looked, but it wasn't my intention to become a bed for this human.

Enola's eyes sparkled, though she made no comment and brought the basket to her workbench. She didn't need to speak. I'd known her long enough to understand her thoughts, which mirrored my own.

Why was I still holding Rosalie, and why couldn't I bring myself to pull away?

TWELVE

ROSALIE

When I woke, I was in a strange, quaint cottage, packed with flowers, colorful patch worked quilts, the floral scent making me feel like I was inside a garden. A woman in a simple white dress stood by a stove oven, mixing a pot.

I sat up in the bed, blinking back the confusion. Where was I?

"You're awake," the woman said.

"Where am I?"

She took a ladle and scooped out the contents of the pot into a bowl. "My home. Baine brought you here after the crone attacked you."

I shivered at the memory. "How long have I been here?"

"Just a day." She carried the bowl over to me. "Eat."

"Thank you." Taking the bowl, I glanced around the cottage.

"He's not here," she said with a smile. "He went to the lake but should return any minute."

The door opened and Baine walked in. When he saw me, his eyes widened, and the faint hint of a smile played on his lips. "You're awake."

I nodded, too busy eating the soup this gracious woman gave me.

"Good, we need to return."

"I can take the both of you," the woman said. "After you let her eat and have a few minutes to wake."

"Yes, Enola, of course." Baine placed a basket full of fish he'd been carrying on the table. "And your payment."

"Oh." Enola stood, smiling at the trout. "You found the rainbow ones."

"You doubted my skill?"

"Those trout are in deep. I doubted you'd shed all that leather to get me a few fish."

Baine's cheeks seemed to almost shine, and I wondered if he was blushing.

"You wanted rainbow trout as payment and so you got it." He quickly turned away from both of us and focused on the fish in the basket. "I can debone them if you like."

"No, but now that you're here, I can use the outhouse." Enola left, leaving Baine and me alone.

Not knowing what to say, I continued to eat. He sat in the chair next to the bed. Water dripped off his hair and he pushed the wet strands back off his face. Normally, his shaggy silver hair blocked half of his face, but now I could see everything.

My cheeks warmed at the way he stared at me.

"How are you feeling?" he asked, crossing his legs at the ankles as he stretched out on the chair which seemed like a child's seat under his imposing physique.

"Tired. What happened? Where's everyone else?"

He leaned over, holding out a hand and I gave him the empty bowl. "The crone attacked, you fell, and I brought you here."

"Where's here?"

"Enola is a local healer. You needed to be treated, quickly. Crones are very dirty creatures, and their bites can cause terrible infections."

I glanced at my arm. White cotton wrapped around my forearm right where that horrid thing took a bite out of me. I grabbed the bandage and began to unravel it.

"What are you doing?" Baine dropped the

bowl on the floor and put a hand over mine.

"I want to see it."

Understanding filled his gaze and he slid back with a nod. "Careful."

"I know." Taking one end of the bandage, I slowly undid the wrapping.

Black thread stitched the oval wound closed. The skin surrounding the bite had become an angry shade of red and circled out like a terrible infection. My fingers shook as I traced the stitching.

"You'll be fine," Baine reassured. "Enola is one of the best."

I thought back to the crone. It knew what I was. I didn't know how, but it did. Knowing that creature knew my secret upset me more than the bite on my arm.

"What do you know about crones?" Baine asked.

Ignoring the way Baine studied my face, I took the bandage and re-wrapped my arm. "Nothing. What are they?"

"Creatures who eat magic."

My fingers shook. "Oh, that's morbid."

Baine slid forward on the chair and took the bandage out of my hands and began wrapping it around my arm. "They rarely go after anything living, unless the power levels are immensely high."

My throat became dry, and the room heated. I needed air. "That's interesting. Can I get some water?"

Holding my arm, Baine forced me to face him. His lavender gaze seemed to see right through me, deep inside to all the secrets I held. "What are you?"

"Just a woman."

The silence spread between us. He held on to me, staring, forcing me to speak my truth, but I wouldn't, not for him, not for anyone.

"I feel much better!" Enola swung open the door. "Are you two ready?"

For one moment, Baine eyed me, before letting go of my arm and standing. "We are. I'll wait outside."

And just like that he disappeared out the door, leaving me with a ton of questions.

"How are you feeling?" Enola smiled and carried over a simple white dress with blue stitching along the bodice and hem.

"Okay. Thank you."

She placed the dress on the bed. "Here's a fresh outfit. Once you're ready, we can leave."

"Is there somewhere I can wash? I need a few moments."

"Of course." She pointed out the window. "The lake is right outside. There's a spot behind the waterfall where you can wash your hair. The cave has an overhang and the water rushes over it."

She reached over to a side table and opened the drawer. "Here's some plum and vanilla soap."

Taking the soap, I held it to my chest and stood. "Thank you. I won't be long."

Outside, Baine rested against a cart hitched to a goat, though the goat seemed bigger than any goat I'd seen before. Baine lifted his gaze to me and before he could ask me a thousand questions, I scurried off toward the lake.

I needed to be alone and make sense of what happened.

The sound of rushing water moved me forward, desperate for a moment alone. Something screeched overhead and I looked up into the shimmery sky to see a beautiful white hawk fly overhead.

When my brother left, he had promised to earn enough coin and return, but that never happened. Months passed and I'd spent everything we had on medicine for the firehawks. The old ranger who watched my flock now thought maybe they were sick from bacteria in the feed or the water. When that didn't work, I'd gone to the bank, borrowing coin, and paying any healer in the North who could help.

No one knew what was wrong or how to fix it. And each day the plague snakes infected more of the land.

If only my twin were here to talk to. He always seemed to understand and make sense out of terrible situations. He would know what to do. I couldn't marry and I couldn't escape. I needed a solution, and quickly.

Failing this idiotic competition meant I'd be sent off to spend three years working off my debt. My home would be destroyed by then.

Shaking off the dismal thoughts in my mind, I continued walking to where Enola said I could bathe.

Ahead, the waterfall plunged from high in the cliff rock. So high I couldn't see the top from here on the ground. The mist created rainbows across the stone. Following the path behind the waterfall, I found the hidden area Enola spoke of. On the floor to the right by the cavern walls rested a wooden bucket and a brush. Eager to get this stench and dirt off me, I shimmied out of my dress. Taking the bucket, I moved to the area at the front where a sheet of water hid me from view.

I stuck out my foot just enough that the water splashed my toes.

Oh, it's warm.

With a sigh, I stuck my head under the

rushing water and washed my hair. Back home we didn't have spectacular waterfalls or magical skies, but we did have majestic mountains and rivers that roared with life.

After I had thoroughly rubbed the soap over every inch of my body, I rinsed and slipped into the soft cotton dress. The simple frock fit perfectly and constricted nothing. A dress I could breathe in. I'd have to thank Enola.

I dropped the soap in the bucket and left the hidden cave.

Baine sat on the grass, staring out over the lake. His black assassin type gear may have looked out of place among the pink and white flowers, but not his expression. He seemed relaxed.

Not wanting to disturb his moment of peace, I tiptoed across the grass. His head turned, almost immediately, meeting my gaze head on.

"Hi." I gave a little wave.

He went to stand, and I patted the air, making him stay. "Don't. Sit with me for a minute."

With a nod, he turned and rested an arm across his bent knee. Out under this mystical sky, the sun highlighted the warm plum hues of his skin. The purple undertones made the lavender in his eyes brighten, and those tiny flecks of pink around his pupils gave him the prettiest eyes in all of Saol.

Sitting next to him, I smiled. “It’s beautiful here.”

“It is,” he said, the hard lines of his face softening. “Do you know why they call it the Moonlake?”

I shook my head.

“When the moon is at its fullest, it shines onto the water and the luminescent rocks along the bottom of the lake light up. I’ve never seen anything close to that beauty.”

He turned when he said those last words, eyeing me with an intense gaze that made my toes curl. We were sitting only a few inches apart, the edge of my dress brushing up against his hip.

“What do you want?” he asked.

“Huh?” The question jarred me almost as much as the way he eyed me with this insatiable hunger.

“Is it only your family’s farm you want to save?”

A dragonfly flew over to us and landed on Baine’s arm. It fluttered iridescent wings and seemed to think Baine was a pretty resting spot.

I didn’t disagree.

“Rosalie.”

Hearing him say my name made my palms sweat and my heart flutter as fast as those dragonfly wings.

"It's not just my farm in danger."

"What do you mean?" His body shifted toward me, almost as if he was truly eager to hear my story.

"About two years ago, these snakes appeared out of nowhere. Black slimy things that secrete poison from the glands when they feed. That poison has been destroying our soil, affecting other animals. It's almost as if these snakes are creating a plague, hence the name." Seeing how he watched me speak, urged me to tell him more. "My firehawks hunt these snakes and we were so close to complete eradication . . . but then they got sick. I . . . I think they're dying."

The insect casually sunning itself on Baine stilled.

When Baine didn't respond, I cursed myself for being too open with him, but decided to keep talking. "I can't go away for three years. Do you think Lord Demious will help my home if I marry him? He has to know a way to save the hawks and remove the snakes, right?"

"What if there was another way?"

"What do you mean? Another way for what?"

Instead of answering, Baine examined the dragonfly on his arm before the bug took flight and disappeared. Baine's gaze followed the insect, watching it zip across the water.

"You don't belong in captivity," he said.

"Captivity? Is that what you think of marriage?" I laughed. He didn't.

Gazing over at me with long full eyelashes, he continued, "Marrying Lord Demious will remove your debt and you can pay to hire someone to take care of your farm or bring your firehawks here once the problem is solved, but you'll never be allowed to leave Farrow's Gate."

"It's pretty here. I don't think I would mind staying," I joked, feeling unsettled by Baine's comments.

"After you've been in your cage long enough, you'll believe that."

Why was Baine so concerned about my life or what happened? "What does it matter to you? I'm just a prospect."

"You're much more than that."

I gaped at him, surprised by his words. Was it because he knew about my magic or had a feeling about it? Were fae sympathizers of other races?

Baine stood and held out his hand. "We need to leave."

Taking it, I let him help me to my feet. "What's the other way?"

With his hand still wrapped in mine, he said, "I've worked for Lord Demious for a long time and have quite a bit of coin saved."

"No. Absolutely not." I ripped my hand out of

his. "I'm not taking your money."

He frowned. "But you will marry or be a slave for it?"

"That's different."

Folding his arms, his frown deepened.

"I'm not taking your money," I said, turning on my heel and moving back to Enola's house. "End of discussion."

"Would you take an investment?"

I stopped, my body heating with frustration.

His steps sounded closer until I knew he was standing right behind me. "I would be willing to invest my coin into your firehawks."

Would he? Could I? "And Lord Demious would just allow you to do that for me?"

"Let me worry about Lord Demious. This is a better solution, and one that will set you free from any debt." His voice lowered. "Consider it."

"Why? Why does it matter to you so much?"

The closeness of his body to mine sent my heart into a tailspin, and I knew he had to hear it with that fae hearing of his.

"You remind me of someone."

"Who?"

"Me."

He whispered the word near my ear before walking past, leaving me breathless. I wanted to know how I reminded him of himself. I wanted to know where our similarities lay. Was it deep, almost animalistic? Was it the fact we both belonged under the sky with the grass between our toes? Or was it something emotional? I didn't know about his past or his family. What happened to him? And how did he end up in Farrow's Gate?

By the time we reached Enola's she was sitting on the bench in the wagon cart, reins in hand, and feeding her goat a bundle of herbs. "That dress suits you well."

"Thank you." I smiled and slid my hands down the sides and pretended I didn't notice Baine watching me.

"Get in," Enola said. "I'll have you back by sunset."

Baine jumped into the back of the wooden cart, which was extremely small. How would the both of us fit? He leaned over and held out his hand, which I took.

"Umm." I looked around at the three-foot-wide space.

Baine sat and stretched out his arms along the edge of the cart. "Sit."

"Where?"

He glanced down at his lap, and I swear my face turned bright red. "Okay."

I sat on his legs, and he grunted.

"Sorry," I said in a hushed tone. "There's not

a lot of room here."

With a quick swipe of his arm, he grabbed me by the waist and pulled me on to his lap, holding me back against him. I froze, not knowing what to do with my hands, my feet, my head.

"Relax," he said. "It's a long ride and you'll be more comfortable this way."

With that he leaned back his head, closing his eyes, arm still wrapped around my waist. The cart began moving and I did the only thing I could, lean back into the fae holding me and watch the landscape pass us by.

THIRTEEN

BAINE

Within minutes of me feigning sleep, Rosalie rested against my shoulder and dozed off. It wasn't until she curled into my arm and her chest rose and fell that I opened my eyes. If I hadn't pretended to sleep the girl would have fussed and moved about until the both of us were more than uncomfortable.

And I did not mind her resting in my arms.

"You know Demious will take her," Enola said from the front. "How he hasn't sensed her power already is surprising. The man is getting distracted in his old age."

"The collars dampen the prospects' abilities." I traced a finger around the jeweled choker on

Rosalie's neck.

"Well, he'll learn once he finds out what the crone tried to do."

"He won't."

Enola peered over her shoulder at me. I could only make out the side of her face from this angle, but I could tell she wasn't going to let the conversation drop. "And why won't he?"

"I've offered Rosalie a way out. She doesn't need to marry him. Her debt will be paid."

"Since when do you care about us lowly humans?"

Rosalie nuzzled against my shirt. A low whistling noise came out of her mouth as she snored. "I care about you."

"Oh, do you?" Enola's voice pitched up and I could tell she was smiling. "I'm flattered."

"Why are you so interested in what happens to this woman?" I asked.

"Because you are, of course. I don't think I've ever seen you interested in much of anything."

There were many things that interested me, but my wants died many years ago. My life became a weapon, used when needed. Nothing else seemed to matter and I was fine with it, until this human crashed into my life.

Holding Rosalie in my arms, I realized the danger she stirred in my heart. A need to protect. If I could save her from a life of servitude, I would. The reason why didn't matter.

Lord Demious saved me, and out of duty and honor I served him and would continue to do so until he passed into the Never. Rosalie wasn't here out of loyalty, but a debt that needed to be paid and a home that needed saving.

If I hadn't seen the glow on her face the day those ash raptors plucked her off the grass and into the sky, I may not have believed her desire to save her farm and her firehawks. I may not have known the human woman long, but I understood her need to protect things that mattered, like I once did a long time ago.

Often, I had asked myself if I regretted my decision to save the human children. Was it worth being exiled from my kind? Was it worth losing my home and family? In all the years I'd been in Farrow's Gate my answer remained the same: yes.

Once, Lord Demious had offered to relieve me of my services, but I refused. I had no home to go to, and no desire to do anything else but fight. Until now.

"Dark clouds ahead," Enola said. "Need to speed it up or we'll get stuck in the storm."

Shifting my body to the right, I turned. Across the plains and windy dirt road, gray clouds hovered in the distance, blasts of lightning crackled within their dark mists. Our destination swerved left of the storm, but at the rate we were moving we would meet those clouds head on.

"Can your goat go any faster?"

With a quirk to her lip, Enola said, "This is a Moonlake goat. He may be as fast as you. Hold on!"

With a tap of the reins and a yell, Enola urged the goat forward. Keeping one arm around Rosalie, I grabbed the edge of the cart. The wooden cart bounced along the road, hitting every rock and bramble with a thud. Rosalie squeaked awake, eyes wide with fear, and gripped the front of my shirt.

"What's going on?" She gazed around us, searching for the threat that had awoken her from sleep.

"Storm," I said over the thundering.

Slipping out of my grip, she turned and pulled herself closer to the side of the cart. "What are rainstorms like in Farrow's Gate?"

The cart bounced, jostling us on top of each other. Untangling myself from Rosalie's arms, I slid to squeeze next to her as best as I could. "Depends on the weather."

She opened her mouth to say something, but the boom of thunder roared over her. Placing my hand on her side, I leaned closer to her ear. "Don't be afraid. We'll reach the estate before the storm reaches us."

Rain began pouring from the sky in heavy sheets. No warning, no time to react. Rosalie lifted her arms above her head trying to cover herself. "You were saying?"

Water covered her face, drowning her hair and the dress she wore. I pulled off my shirt and moved to hold it above her head to shield her. The rain soaked the shirt by the time I had it above Rosalie's face.

She laughed.

I laughed.

And then something odd happened.

I laughed again.

Rosalie grabbed the shirt and tossed it at me, her smile wide and beautiful. She lifted her arms up to the sky, face tilted to meet the rain head on. Water droplets slid down her cheeks, slicking her long red hair to the sides of her face. She swayed side to side, opening her mouth to drink the raindrops.

Thunder and lightning met in the sky above us, igniting the storm and drumming a beat to match the tempo of my heart. It was in that loud, chaotic moment, I knew exactly why I had decided to save this precious human.

FOURTEEN

ROSALIE

Maybe it was because fae were legendary creatures, but when Baine laughed it changed *everything*. Not just his face, that would be too normal. It changed the world around him. The air smelled fresher, the storm not as terrifying, and even though the sun wasn't visible, I could feel those warm rays against my chest.

When we stopped laughing, his expression shifted and he leaned over, almost close enough to feel his breath hit my face. Rain splashed on our faces, droplets running down his slender nose. Nothing could ever be more beautiful than the fae in front of me.

"When we arrive," he yelled over the storm.

"I'll explain to Lord Demious what happened. He doesn't need to know the crone tried to feed on you."

Baine was going to lie for me?

"My offer still stands," he continued. "If you wish, I will pay your debt and you'll be free to go home to your farm. Enola may even know a way to help your firehawks."

"Come with me!"

The words left my mouth before I could think. I don't know why I said them, and based on his shocked expression, he didn't know why either. Trying to fix the utter foolishness, I quickly thought of a reason.

"If it's an investment, you should see what your coin is paying for."

If he didn't believe my excuse for saying something so ridiculous, he saved me the embarrassment by not calling me out. "My life is here."

But it could be somewhere else.

Through the pouring rain, Baine watched me. Water danced across his cheekbones which were painfully beautiful at this distance. And those eyes. How did a fae end up with pink lavender eyes and eyelashes too pretty for a male?

I wanted him to say something, *anything*. Instead, I was met with thunder, rain, and the occasional bleat of a goat.

Why did Baine want to help me? I had to know.

But I wouldn't get that chance, not today.

Enola turned into the estate, passing through the shimmering shield and massive black iron gates. My collar buzzed, heating my neck. I shoved my fingers in between my skin and the metal to ease the pain.

"Are you all right?" Baine shouted, even though he really didn't need to at this distance. He held my arm, gaze panning my neck. "It should stop now that we're past the barrier. Lord Demious had adjusted the spell on the barrier to let the prospects back in after we left yesterday."

While the buzzing stopped, the slight burn of metal irritated my skin and I kept trying to shove a finger in to ease the pain. Baine's brow furrowed as he watched me squirm with the uncomfortable sensation.

When we hit a large rock in the road, the cart bounced, and I went up and down hard on my bum.

"Oh, that's going to hurt in the morning," I cried.

Baine's hand stayed on my arm, and that odd look of concern tormented his face.

"What's wrong?" I asked.

He quickly removed his hand as if he just realized he'd been touching me this whole time. "Nothing. Are you sure you're all right?"

This time I touched him.

Taking his hand in mine, I smiled. "I will be."

Instead of returning my smile, Baine looked away from me. "Remember what we discussed."

"Remember what I said." Squeezing his hand within mine, I searched his face for some hint of emotion, anything to explain what I was feeling, what *he* was feeling.

He gave me nothing.

The cart stopped outside the mansion and guards ran to meet us.

"Baine!" A fae with the same plum skin as Baine ran up to us. "Is everything okay?"

Baine nodded. "The prospect is safe. How is Lord Demious?"

The fae frowned. "Crankier than usual. He's been asking for you. Better go see him."

"I will." Baine turned to Enola and held out a hand to help her down, which she brushed aside. "Stay here tonight. I'll see the goat is taken care of. It's too dangerous to travel now."

Enola patted Baine's chest. "Very well. I might as well go visit my old friend when you're done with him."

Even completely soaked, Enola was stunning. Her long gray hair hung around her shoulders, and her bright eyes simmered with life. She placed her hands on my arms and smiled. "You take care."

"Thank you, for everything," I said.

She looked at Baine then to me. "Take care of him. He's not as tough as he seems."

Baine frowned and I held back a laugh. Somehow, I believed Enola understood Baine better than he did. She patted my shoulder and shuffled inside the mansion.

"I'll bring you to your room," Baine said and walked toward the front door.

There was no reason to feel nervous, yet my heart would not stop fluttering in my chest. Though we walked in silence, the air seemed filled with unspoken words. He walked beside me, close but not too close.

His boots squeaked against the marble floor.

My heart beat a fast *thump thump*.

Once, I peeked over at him, only to find his jaw tight and gaze focused ahead.

When he stopped at my door it felt like the end of something.

Why wasn't I ready to say goodbye?

"Is there anything you need?" he asked.

Looking up at his face, I wanted to say what was on my mind, in my heart, but I couldn't. There was no way I could explain this strange emotion and how I wanted to spend another day figuring it out.

"Rosalie!" Ara's voice broke through the silence, and she ran over to me, her navy bow flopping side to side on top of her head. "Are you all right? We've been so worried."

"I'm fine."

"Oh, you are soaked." She grabbed my arm. "I'll run you a hot bath and you can get out of those wet clothes."

Baine's gaze met mine and this time I knew exactly what kind of thoughts ran through that mind of his. His light eyes darkened, and his jaw twitched.

"Thank you for keeping her safe, Baine." Ara tugged me inside.

"Goodbye," I said to him, and when he looked at me with a sorrowful expression, I suddenly didn't want him to go.

FIFTEEN

BAINE

Marco leaned up against the table, staring down at the map of the estate. "Patrol last night found another dead animal here and here."

Two black marks notated areas on the map, one was in the perimeter of the mansion, the other far at the south side of the estate in the middle of the orchard. A massive iron gate surrounded the orchard to keep the wandering animals out which made it odd that anything was found inside.

"Tell me what happened at the orchard."

"Dead birds."

"How many?"

"Four, maybe five, not a lot but they were all

around the same area, but there's more." Marco scratched the back of his head, a nervous tick he had whenever something unsettled him. "There were eaten apples by the birds."

"Eaten by what?"

He got up and walked over to a satchel hanging on the hook near the door. He opened it up and took out an apple core then tossed me the fruit.

Birds didn't have the physical ability to make bites like this. The teeth marks around the apple could only be made by one creature. "Someone is sneaking out at night."

"Impossible. One of the patrols would have noticed."

I dropped the apple on the table. "There's no lock on the gate. It's only to keep animals out."

"I got a bad feeling about this. Dead birds? We haven't had anything like this on the estate in over a decade. Bringing all that magic here is like lighting a beacon to every monster close by."

"I'm going to patrol."

"It's pouring out."

After leaving my weapons by the door, I opened it. "Keep watch over the mansion. Make sure no one leaves."

"Where are you going?"

"Hunting." With that I shifted and stepped

out into the pelting rain.

My paws sunk into the mud, and I lifted my muzzle, inhaling the earthy scent of the storm. Thunder boomed in the night sky, the sound drowning out Marco's grumbling about dinner. He'd moved into the dining area of the barracks where the guards ate.

Launching into a run, I sprinted toward the orchard, letting my animalistic senses take over. Water drenched my fur but did nothing to slow me down. If darkthings had entered the grounds, their foul stench would be easy to pick up in this form.

The world passed by in shades of shifting gray. Lightning crackling in the sky provided the only form of light, which was more than enough for what I needed. I was the only wolf on the estate, and the biggest predator here. Lord Demious had cleansed the grounds many years before after my arrival, and only docile animals were allowed in the area.

Memories of Rosalie being taken by ash raptors flickered in my thoughts. The creatures were not aggressive by nature, which made their behavior odd. What had they been trying to do with her? Were they connected to what was happening on the estate?

I shook my head, jarring the image of Rosalie out. I couldn't think about her now. My duty to keeping the estate safe came first.

A coppery scent hit my nose, and I slid to a stop. Slowly, I eyed the area, watching for shadows and movement then stalked toward the metallic aroma cautiously. The smell intensified and I could make out a large shape huddled on the ground.

Using my keen hearing, I listened to the storm, paying attention to the lightest sound that echoed within it. When I was only met with the rain and thunder, I stalked the lump on the grass.

Dark liquid pooled beneath the mass. The closer I came, I could decipher the distinct outline of a human arm laid out, the rest of the body covered with a cloak. I nudged the hand with my nose.

Ice cold.

No pulse, no breath.

Blood covered the dirty fingertips.

I bit the edge of the cloak and tugged, rolling the body forward.

A young woman, eyes open and staring out in horror, had half of her neck torn out. Long, jagged scrapes covered the neck down to the front of her dress, which had been shredded. The plain servant outfit signified she was one of ours. Off to the side, smashed and broken, a wicker basket sat, apples strewn out beside her.

In the distance, the iron gate to the orchard swung back and forth. I followed the trail of blood to the entrance, but any signs of what had attacked her were gone. No sounds, no other scent but the old blood. Going back to the body, I shifted back into human form and kneeled next to the dead servant. Out of the gifts Lord Demious had given me, the bracelet that allowed me to shift and keep my clothes had been the most convenient.

With my finger, I closed her eyes. Based on the scent of her blood and temperature of her skin, she'd been dead for about twelve hours. Wrapping the cloak around her body, I lifted her and began the trek back to the estate. Lord Demious would need to know about this and quickly.

Using my swiftness, I returned to the barracks, calling out to Marco. When he saw what I carried, his eyes went wide. I placed the girl on the floor.

He stared at the covered body. "Who is it?"

"One of the maids. I'm going to get Lord Demious."

Marco opened his mouth, but I disappeared before he could ask any more questions. If there was something out on the grounds killing our people, why couldn't I find it? The trail simply wasn't there.

Inside the manor, I went to Lord Demious' study. He had a thing for storms and liked to watch them from his balcony, preferably with a glass of honey wine.

I knocked on his door, making sure I wiped any blood on my hands off on my pants.

"Who is it?" he said, and I heard a giggle. He had a female in there with him.

"Baine. It's important."

"You may enter."

Candlelight flickered off the mahogany walls. Lord Demious laid on his chaise lounge, a woman curled against his side. The balcony doors were slightly opened, making the black velvet curtains swing with the wind. He lifted his glass and sipped as the female nibbled on his neck. Her back faced me, making it difficult to see who he had brought into his room.

"Have you been playing in the rain?" With his free hand he stroked the female's dark hair and she curled into him, her mouth moving to his ear.

"We need to speak, alone," I said. Without knowing who was in his lap, I couldn't risk the danger of what I was about to say.

"Surely it can wait," he replied, moving his hand down the female's back until it grazed her waist. "I'm otherwise engaged."

The female slid her arm around his neck and

whispered in his ear. He laughed and I could tell I would need to be more direct than I cared for.

"We have a security breach."

All humor left his face. "Leave us."

The human kissed his cheek before sliding off his lap. She stood, fixing the front of her dress which had been slightly pulled down.

Claudia.

The eldest of the Haalow sisters. She smiled at me, licking her lips, before glancing to Lord Demious and placing a hand on his shoulder. "Remember what I said."

He nodded and eyed her with a look I knew too well. If he hadn't bedded her already, he would. "We *will* continue this later."

Satisfied, she left.

I closed the door behind her. "I see you've made your choice."

"Not yet, but I do like that one very much. We have similar . . . tastes." He finished the rest of his drink in one gulp and slammed his glass on the table. "What happened?"

"Better if I show you."

Taking a cloak from the coat rack, he pulled up the hood and followed me outside into the storm and to the barracks. When we arrived, Marco was pacing in front of the body.

Lord Demious kneeled on the floor, the hood

of his cloak falling back. He unraveled the cloak covering the body, revealing the dead girl's face. Marco cursed and punched the wall. He was much closer to the servants than I was. I'd kept my distance from everyone, except my men and Lord Demious.

"Meryl," Lord Demious said with a sigh. "Sweet girl. Where did you find her?"

"By the orchard, she's been dead no more than twelve hours. I found no trace or trail of what creature did this."

"How did this happen?" Marco continued pacing. "The barrier keeps everything out of the estate and there hasn't been any attack like this in Farrow's Gate for years."

Lord Demious leaned closer, examining the gashes across Meryl's body. His brow knitted together before he covered the girl back up and stood. "No one must know about this attack. Bury her tonight and I'll tell the servants that she fell and broke her neck while picking apples."

Marco scrunched his face, and I could tell he was about to say something he'd regret. "My lord, this security breach means danger to anyone here. Call off this competition and send the females home. Marry Claudia and be done with it."

"No, this only proves the importance of finding a powerful female to carry my lineage.

The barrier, and not just here, but surrounding all of Farrow's Gate is powered by my magic. If it is waning, it means the darkness from the Never is corroding more than we know. Your men need to comb these grounds until you find me that darkthing."

"So, it is a darkthing," I said, meeting his gaze. "Most of those creatures are not intelligent. Wouldn't it still be attacking?"

"The darkthing isn't the issue. They don't attack and disappear, and yes there are some denizens from the Never that have a mind of their own, but those are extremely rare. This is an attack, and we need to find out from who."

"Wait." Marco held a hand to his forehead. "You're saying someone is summoning this thing?"

Lord Demious' brow furrowed. "If that is possible, we're in greater danger than I thought."

"Who would do such a thing?" Lord Demious had enemies, but it had been years since any surfaced.

Folding his arms, the magistrate stared at the dead girl. "In desperate times, men will do desperate things. If Saol is destined to fall, Farrow's Gate may be the only safe haven left."

"Wait, what?" Marco's eyes widened. "You can't mean that? The war is not even near here."

Grabbing my weapons off the floor, I belted

my swords back on, Lord Demious' words sending an uneasiness through me. "You know something."

Marco glanced back between Lord Demious and me.

With a sigh, Lord Demious met my gaze, his expression hardening. "The war with the Never Rift has come to a head, and only one side will prevail. We must all play our part, and I will do as I must."

With a whirl of his cloak, he left the barracks, Marco's eyes widening and his mouth opening to spew a thousand questions I didn't have answers to.

The magistrate knew something, and I had a sense we were all in grave danger.

SIXTEEN

ROSALIE

All of us stood near a ring outside with target dummies in the center. Lord Demious walked into the middle, wearing that grand smile of his. His long red and black coat flapped in the wind.

"Good morning, ladies," he said. "Today, we will test your magical abilities. Each one of you will step into this ring where I will remove your collar and you will be allowed to showcase your talent. As I have said before, my bride will need to exhibit powerful magic. Remember, you will be a ruler of Farrow's Gate and your lineage will keep this land safe."

Whispers and excitement buzzed around us. I admitted. I was curious to see what the other girls were able to do, especially that trio to my left. The sisters huddled together, conversing. Claudia glared at me. Today, she wore a ruby dress that tied in the front, pushing her breasts up, making them seem bigger than they really were. She may have been prettier than me, but no bodice would ever get her chest to be as big as mine.

It was a silly thing to be proud of, but I was. I liked my curves, and I didn't need to be constricted to death to show them off.

"Where have you been? I've been so worried." Janetta moved next to me and hugged me. "They wouldn't tell us anything except that you were hurt and needed to rest. I've been in a panic ever since you disappeared."

"I'm okay," I whispered, squeezing her back. "I'll explain everything later, I promise."

Ms. Begalia clapped, forcing the conversation to end.

"Alicia," Lord Demious said. "Step forward."

Alicia walked into the ring. Her white dress blended with her pale hair and skin tone making her ghost like. Lord Demious waved a hand in front of her collar, and it fell into his hands. At the same time, an iridescent bubble rose around the ring, encasing the two inside.

"Proceed," he said, and moved to the edge of the ring.

This is what all of us had been waiting for. The

real reason each of us were even considered.

I held my breath, waiting to see Alicia's power.

She took one step and vanished.

All of us gasped, except Lord Demious who stood with a focused gaze on the spot Alicia left. Moments later, she reappeared right next to the dummy.

"A shadow walker." Demious' expression tightened, and I didn't miss the quick glance he gave Baine. "There are very few people who can shadow walk. Alec failed to mention your unique ability."

Quickly, Lord Demious placed the collar back on her neck, not waiting for a response. "You may return to the others."

With a flick of his wrist, the shield around the ring lowered, letting Alicia out. She glanced back at the ring and her expression fell. Was she hoping to impress the magistrate? He didn't seem pleased with her ability.

"Claudia." Lord Demious called the oldest sister of the trio forward.

She sauntered into the ring, a cocky smile on her lips. Her black hair swayed with her steps, and there was no doubting the desire in Demious' gaze when he watched her.

He removed her collar, and the session started.

Suddenly, there were three Claudias in the

ring.

"Illusionary. Good." Lord Demious walked around the clones. "But nothing extraordinary."

Claudia scowled at the comment and lifted her hands.

The ring went black.

Guards ran forward, and Janetta and I looked at each other.

A moment later, the darkness receded, and Lord Demious laughed.

"You've made your point, Claudia. Well done." He put the collar back on and whispered in her ear. Whatever he said made her smile as her face lit and she hurried back to her sisters.

On and on the exercises went. Most of the girls had similar arcane abilities, only one had the power to summon a creature—Lord Demious thoroughly enjoyed that, but my favorite was watching Janetta.

She explained to Demious that she couldn't practice her ability without hurting someone or something, and she didn't want to do that. He brought over flowers and Janetta spewed a poison cloud from her mouth all over the roses, wilting them in an instant.

But me . . . he saved me for last.

As I headed to the ring, I glanced around for Baine, but he had disappeared at some point. Yesterday had been strange and I wasn't sure what to make of any of it. I wanted to talk to him more.

"Good afternoon, Rosalie." Demious removed my collar.

The flame sparked inside me, warming my body, and making me feel whole again. I had to show him something, but not too much. After Baine's declaration, I knew I didn't have to marry or be a slave. Of course, I couldn't act like that. No, I had to pretend to want to win.

Slowly, I created a ball of fire in my palms.

"Surely, you can do more?" Demious hovered near me. "Attack that dummy."

The dummy had a crude helmet and consisted of burlap bags of stuffed hay. I faced the dummy and focused on the fire. Once I had the flame in my grasp, I visualized it releasing through my fingers and at the target.

Someone clapped, probably Janetta, and I glanced to see Lord Demious nod his approval. Being able to use fire magic wasn't that uncommon. I hoped that display would be enough to appease him.

Demious snapped the collar back on, snuffing my flame into darkness once again. I ran out of the ring to Janetta who practically bounced on her feet.

"You're the strongest here," she whispered.

"No way, poison? That's a talent."

She shrugged and we both stood, waiting for our next instructions.

Lord Demious looked to the estate where a servant waved at him.

And right next to that servant waited a Borderlands Agent. I'd recognize the green and red leathers anywhere. Calvin had left with a man dressed in similar attire.

"Ms. Begalia, take the ladies for afternoon tea." Lord Demious gave a slight bow. "Until tonight."

I didn't know why someone from the Borderlands was here, but I had to find out.

Ms. Begalia called us to attention with that incessant clapping of hers, treating us like a bunch of chicks. The other girls around me whispered and gossiped about the day's events. None of that mattered with a Borderlands Agent here.

Do they know about me? Is it Calvin?

Oh, no, what if it's Calvin?

I can't bear to lose him.

Calvin promised he would not use his full potential in battle. He was simply a common fire mage looking to fight and make coin.

Janetta walked in front of me, and I discreetly whispered in her ear.

"I need to leave. If anyone asks, say I've retired to my room because the magic use exhausted me."

"Is everything okay?"

"I'm not sure."

When the group turned to enter inside, I sprinted toward the entrance I saw Lord Demious and the agent go through. The door opened into a foyer off the drawing room, but I couldn't hear or see anyone. Where would they have gone?

The male servant with the curls walked past, holding a tray of drinks and pastries.

"Hi," I said, waving.

He smiled back. "Good afternoon, milady. Can I help you?"

"I was hoping I could speak privately with Lord Demious." I bit my lip and coyly looked away. "Without the other girls around."

"Oh, of course." He motioned for me to step closer. "He's in his office with a guest, but if you'd like me to arrange a meeting, I can."

"I wouldn't want to disturb him right now. Maybe I can steal a moment later." I gave a slight bow of my head. "Goodbye!"

With my dress in hand, I ran outside, only pausing to make sure no one else was around me. Lord Demious' office was upstairs on the second floor, east wing. I remembered from that first day when I spotted him watching through the window.

I also remembered a gigantic tree near it.

By the time I reached that area of the estate, sweat soaked the back of my neck and pooled in between my breasts. The willow tree was in full bloom with plenty of leaves and purple flowers to give me enough spying coverage. The first branch wasn't too far. I jumped up and grabbed it.

I'm sure those sisters had never climbed a tree in their life. Not only could I climb, but I was better than my brother.

When I pulled myself up onto the first large branch, I grabbed another and began working my way up the tree, branch by branch. My dress snagged on a section of the limb, ripping the hem.

This is ridiculous. I can't climb in this.

I positioned myself on a thick branch and undid the front lace of my bodice then shimmied out of my dress. If anyone saw me in my bloomers, I'd be the main gossip for the rest of the time here.

At least I wore underthings today, but only because the twins made me—apparently, going without them is socially unacceptable.

The voices inside grew louder.

I grabbed another branch and finished climbing, knocking my dress off the tree in the process. I couldn't worry about that now. I had to hear what was going on in that room.

"How much longer, Demious?"

"You will have them in three days."

Using my arms, I pulled myself forward and laid flat on the branch nearest the open window. The agent stood on the opposite side of Demious' desk.

"I don't see why you prolong this charade. We need to replenish the ranks. Every day the Rift grows, faster than before, and the spell is not complete yet."

Demious dipped a quill into the ink bottle and wrote on a scroll. "Remember, I get first pick. You can have the leftovers."

My heart raced. *First pick? What is he talking about?*

Once Demious finished writing, he waved his hand over the scroll. "As agreed, and now signed."

The agent took the scroll. "The Magi Council will not look kindly at you harboring mages that are needed for war. Your job has been to find us the mages we need."

Demious stood and black misty tentacles began extending from his body. "And I have done so for years. You should remember whose house you are in. I alone protect Farrow's Gate, and my heir will need to be powerful to keep the mess the Magi Council has made at the Borderlands from defiling the rest of Saol."

The agent stepped back. "The Magi Council pays you to protect it. A fact you seem to forget."

Black tentacles shot forth and wrapped around the agent's neck. Demious' calm demeanor morphed into a sinister smirk and his brown eyes shifted to black. "Go back to town and when I have chosen my bride, you'll get the rest."

The mist receded, and the agent ran out.

My heart pounded.

He's sending the losers to the Borderlands? That's a war zone.

The girls here weren't fighters, they were mages at best.

Demious stormed out of his office.

I shimmied back to the trunk and began climbing my way down.

At that exact moment, Baine walked under the tree. I paused, knowing his acute hearing would find me. He picked up my dress then glanced around. When he didn't see any naked ladies, he looked up.

At me.

I froze, mid-climb.

His eyes widened in shock.

Normally, I'd be mortified about being caught in my underthings, but not after what I'd heard. Ignoring all sense of manners, I hurried down the tree.

"I'll take that," I said and snatched my dress out of Baine's hands.

"What are you doing out here, like that?" he hissed.

"It doesn't matter. I—"

Our conversation was interrupted by the clamoring of feet. Baine swept me into his arms and took off into the woods. Again, my head swayed from the movement. When he finally put me down, I kneeled on the ground to center myself.

Digging my hands into the dirt, I recalled everything Demious had said.

He would choose one, and the rest would be sacrificed to the Borderlands. To death and war. The only reason my brother had a chance of survival was because of our heritage. None of those girls would survive.

What if he sends me?

"Rosalie." Baine spoke my name in a soft tone, placing a hand on my back as he crouched beside me. "What's happened?"

"I . . ." It dawned on me that Baine might be aware of Demious' plans and this whole banter had been a ploy to find out more about me, to see if I was worthy of marriage or death. "Did you know about us?"

"What do you mean?"

I stood, needing to get away from him. My hands trembled as the idea of Baine's offer and his kind words had all been a ruse. Some wicked game to trick me into revealing more about myself. "Did you know what his plans are for the girls he doesn't choose?"

Baine slowly rose, his stoic face giving me nothing. "You'll be sent to work off your debts."

"Do you know where?" My voice rose and fear and anger whirled inside me, shaking me to my core.

"Somewhere in Farrow's Gate."

"No, you're wrong." My chest tightened with worry and fear. "You really don't know?"

My hands trembled as I replayed Demious words over and over. Pulling at the ends of my hair, I paced back and forth, my heartbeat pounding in my ears.

"Were you spying on Lord Demious?"

In that one question, I wasn't sure I could trust Baine and that truth broke my heart. "Please, take me back now."

"What did you hear?" Baine moved closer and I stepped back, hugging the dress to my chest.

Fae were known for their ferocity and loyalty. Baine was a living, breathing legendary creature, dedicated to his master. I knew nothing of his past or how he ended up here. What if his heart was the same black as those tentacles? What if his flirtatious banter had been a trick? Surely, being Lord Demious' most trusted guard, Baine would have to know about us. How could he not?

"Rosalie." Baine's face softened and he held his hands up. "I would not harm you nor see you befall to harm. If you know something, please tell me."

Please, such a simple word and yet that is the one thing that gives me pause.

"I'm afraid," I said in a shaky voice, tears welling in my eyes.

Baine closed the space between us and placed his hands on my arms. "Tell me what frightens you."

"Whoever is not chosen to be his bride will be sent to the Borderlands."

Baine's gaze narrowed. "You heard him say this?"

"Yes, Baine. Anyone who goes there will die! This competition was never about finding the perfect bride. He's been sending mages to the war for years."

"Then make sure he chooses you."

"What?" I wiggled my way out of Baine's grip, shocked at his callous response. "No, that's not the answer! And I'm the last girl he would choose!"

I turned my back to Baine.

How can he say that? These girls and possibly me could die.

"You're wrong," he said behind me. "He senses what I sense. You are something more than a human girl with a bit of fire magic. Even without knowing what the crone did, Lord Demious is no fool. If you show him, you'll be saved."

The sun beamed high in the sky. If I didn't return soon, someone might notice, and suddenly I was tired. Slipping the dress back on, and not caring one bit about my audience, I stared at the woods, remembering what my father made me swear all those years ago.

"No one must know the truth."

"But why, Poppa? Calvin and I are strong. We can protect ourselves."

He picked me up and placed me on his lap. "One day the world will need you and your brother. You are unique. The Magi Council will take you, separate you both from each other and us and do whatever they wish. You must never show anyone what you can do. What you and your brother can really do."

"Okay."

"Promise me, Rosalie."

"I promise, Poppa. No one will find out."

The pain of my parents passing hit me in the chest, making the warm sun feel constricting instead of comforting. They died to keep our power a secret. Instead of using their magic to save themselves from the wildfire, they died inside it.

I couldn't betray them now. I wouldn't. No matter what. Their death would not be in vain. I'd find a way to save myself and these girls without my secret. My parents gave me more than magic. They bestowed on me a mind with the power to think myself out of a bad situation.

"Take me back," I said. "I need to lie down."

Baine placed a hand on my shoulder, stepping close behind me. "My offer still stands. I could sway him to another female and get you out of here before the others are sent away."

"He won't let that happen. He signed a contract with the Magi Council. Whoever isn't chosen will go to war. He's already bargained our lives away. Now, please, take me back."

Baine swept me into his arms, and this time I wondered if it was the last.

SEVENTEEN

BAINE

If Rosalie told the truth, then Lord Demious was keeping me out of his plans, something he rarely did. While I cared little for the other prospects, the lord's dishonest behavior did not sit well with me, and if what Rosalie said was true, I had to get her out of this place, even if she didn't agree.

At this time of day, the magistrate would be busy issuing decrees and solving minor political cases that haunted Farrow's Gate. When I arrived in the drawing room, he was sitting at his desk, writing.

"How am I supposed to keep the estate safe when you neglect to tell me of an agent of the

Borderlands visiting?"

Lord Demious dipped his quill into the ink bottle. "You worry too much."

I hadn't seen the lord since the previous night when I gave him my report. "Are they here about the darkthings?"

At that he sighed and placed the writing utensil on the desk. "No, but we should talk. Let's walk."

Leaving the drawing room, we headed down the stairs and into the basement where he had a secret lab. Mostly he kept his potions and magical items stored here, but it also held a crystal scrying ball which he used to not only communicate with other lords, but to spy.

"The Never Rift continues to grow every decade." Lord Demious waved his hand over the ball. "See for yourself."

A dark scene began formulating in the mist. A blue wall rippling with magic surrounding the Borderlands and, in its center, a black misty hole that seeped creatures made of the very same mist. Spirits, dead ancients, horrors from another dimension that all races fought against.

"It's bigger," I said, noticing the last time Lord Demious showed me the Rift.

"The Magi Council is gathering magical energies to seal the Rift for good. They spent the last ten years crafting a spell that will work.

It will require an enormous amount of power."

"What does that have to do with you? Are you going there?"

"No. I protect Farrow's Gate."

While I knew the truth about his plans, I feigned ignorance. "Then?"

"The prospects are meant for the Borderlands. I'm testing their abilities."

"Were you ever looking for a bride?"

He scoffed at my words. "Of course. I need a strong lineage to protect Farrow's Gate. If the magi fail, the darkness will continue to consume all life. The Rift into the Never has been opened for too long."

"Those girls are not warriors," I said while staring at the vision displayed before us. "They'll be slaughtered."

Lord Demious waved his hand and the image in the scrying sphere blinked out. "When did you start to care about humans?"

"I care about needless death."

"Ahh, yes. That has always been your soft spot. Ever since I found you trapped by those vile hunters."

Not wanting to relive the memory of that day, I brought the conversation back to the present. He hadn't mentioned who out of the prospects had piqued his interest. "Very well. Which one have you chosen?"

A dark grin crossed his face. "So far I like the idea of having three brides. A man gets bored easily."

"You should see if that's a possibility, first. It's best to test the waters before diving in."

Lord Demious laughed. "Good thinking. I'm going to bathe. Have the sisters prepared and brought to my chambers."

"Very well, my lord." I bowed and left him to his laughter.

If he planned on bathing, I would need to steal the key to the collar now. Since he did not mention Rosalie, he may not choose her at all, and I would not allow her to be sent to the Borderlands and to her death. Knowing what he planned to do with the females, I understood he would never agree to set Rosalie free, even if I did pay her debt, which meant I had to save her.

And I had to do it tonight.

EIGHTEEN

ROSALIE

Ara and Luna had checked on me, followed by Janetta. I couldn't tell her what I discovered, not when I had no solution. I thought of Alicia. A delicate young woman who would wither within minutes at the Borderlands.

Even the Haalow sisters wanted to pay off the debt, not die for it. The youngest, Chloe, was too sweet and innocent for war. I owed nothing to the girls, but I couldn't stomach the truth of knowing what awaited them, and Janetta . . . there had to be a way to stop this.

Moonlight filtered through the sheer curtains blowing in the night breeze. The one lantern I had left lit flickered shadows across the walls.

No matter how much I wanted to sleep, my mind wouldn't rest and all I could think about was the future that awaited all of us.

The estate presented the perfect homestead for anyone. Why did Demious make us do these ridiculous tests and why let us enjoy ourselves? Did he care that most of the women here would die? Why would he act as if this competition to win his eye actually mattered?

Feeling lost, confused, and afraid, I closed my eyes and stilled my thoughts.

All Father, hear my plea.

The last time I prayed was after my parents died. I didn't know why, but I needed guidance, a sign on what to do next.

Do I try and escape? And hope I can survive the pain of crossing the barrier around the estate? The ash raptors couldn't do it, but maybe if I run?

Do I do everything I can to prove I'm chosen and safe?

Could I truly send those girls to war?

A strong wind entered the room and I sat up, fear shivering down my spine. A cloaked figure stepped toward my bed.

I gripped the blanket to my chest. Was it Demious? Had he seen me spying earlier?

The shadow stepped into the ray of moonlight pouring in from the window, revealing my intruder. Baine held a finger to his lips as he crept closer.

"What are you doing here?" I whispered.

He motioned to the large wardrobe where my gowns hung. I tossed the blanket aside. Baine rummaged through the wardrobe until he had a hooded navy cloak and a matching dress.

He handed me the clothes and moved to the window.

Thankfully, the dress slipped on easily, no constricting bodice. Once clothed, I hurried to Baine.

"When I transform, get on my back," he said.

"What? Why?"

"Trust me," he whispered before shifting into the silver haired wolf.

Glancing at the massive beast, I wondered where we were going and why he was in his wolf form. He nudged my belly with his head, urging me to get on.

"All right." Lifting one leg over, I climbed onto his back and grabbed the fur by his neck. "What—"

The words died in my throat as Baine leapt out of the window and we soared through the air. With a silent scream, I closed my eyes and flattened myself on his back, holding his fur in a death grip.

He landed with a thud, surprisingly didn't

kill us, and tore off into the woods.

When Baine used the *other* method, the speed made my head spin, but in wolf form he wasn't as fast. Faster than a normal wolf, but slow enough that I could enjoy the wind on my cheeks and the rushing landscape. Holding on tight, I smiled at the way he flew around the trees and leapt over fallen branches. Graceful, steady, and solid.

I wasn't sure where he was taking me, but I sensed from the direction he was headed, we were going toward the entrance of the estate.

He slowed before coming to a full stop. I slid off his back and watched the fur disappear, replaced by beautiful dark skin. His silver hair hung over his right eye, and I desperately wanted to see his expression.

"How do you transform with your clothes?" I asked.

"Magic. I got tired of shredding everything I owned." He waved a black bracelet on his wrist. "Lord Demious crafted this for me, many years ago."

"Where are we?" I didn't recognize anything special about the area, except the road to the estate in the distance. We were in a little clearing full of swaying white flowers and butterfly bushes. At night the bushes were empty, but during the day tons of butterflies would dot the bush, drinking the nectar from the flowers. This was one of the prettier areas of the estate.

He cupped my cheek with his right hand, staring into my eyes. The sudden touch froze me in place. He slipped his other hand behind my neck, gently brushing against my skin.

"What are you doing?" I managed to say, even though I sort of gasped out the question.

The collar clicked and slid away. I caught the jeweled necklace in my hands.

"What did you do?" I gaped at the collar then at him.

His jaw tightened. "You're free."

"How?"

"It doesn't matter. Take the road and don't stop until you leave Farrow's Gate behind." He shoved a pouch into the inside pocket of my cloak. "There's enough coin in there to get you home."

Was this the sign I asked for? To run and escape?

And what about Baine? There's no way he could get away with setting me free. Lord Demious would have to suspect him. My stomach knotted at the decision. There was only one thing I knew for sure. Lord Demious would not choose Janetta. Her poison ability was a cool trick, but not powerful enough which meant she would be sent away.

"Why would you do this?" I asked, staring at the fae before me, wondering why he would bother with setting me free. I placed a hand on his smooth cheek, and he shivered under my touch. Moonlight danced in his lavender eyes.

"Is it not obvious?"

"No, it's not. Maybe you should—" He cut me off with a kiss.

He pressed those soft lips against mine, and the world melted into the shadows around us. I opened my mouth, letting him in. He tasted of wind and earth, grounding me to this moment. The excitement buzzing through my body took over my thoughts, sending them into a whirlwind where I desperately wanted him to touch the most intimate places, and whisk us away where no one would ever find us.

Digging his hands into my hair, Baine kissed me with urgency. I thought back to that moment in the garden, yearning for delicate touches. Hungrily, I kissed, eager for more than what he was giving. He tugged at my dress, his own desire showcasing in a need to free me from my clothes. I pulled at the back of his neck, forcing him closer.

"Rosalie," he whispered as he cruelly left my lips. "You have to go. It is the only way I can save you, but you must go now."

"No."

He pulled back, frowning. "You could be sent to the Borderlands. Lord Demious is keeping things from me. I will not allow you to be taken."

I wanted so much to go and take him with me. How could I possibly leave after a kiss like that? My wants didn't matter though, not when people's lives were at stake.

"I can't leave knowing that Janetta and Alicia could be in danger. I don't care for the other girls, but that doesn't mean they should die. We have to find a way to save them all."

"I will not risk your life."

My heart swelled at his declaration. "We can save them. I know we can find a way. Now that we know what Lord Demious is planning to do, we can stop it. He trusts you. He'll never suspect anything."

"And you're willing to marry him?"

"He won't choose me." Though I tried to say the words with conviction, I didn't know Lord Demious well enough to understand his wants or desires. "Right?"

"Lord Demious is a complicated man. Though you are the most beautiful prospect, he will want a woman with power to enhance his line."

"Then I'm safe. I won't show him what I can really do." For now, not even Baine could know the truth of my ability.

"And what if he changes his mind?" Baine

said, closing the gap I tried to put between us.

"I'll deal with it."

For one very long moment, we stared at one another, unspoken words flying between us. Warmth fluttered in my stomach, and I wanted to tell him how much I appreciated this gesture, and everything it entailed.

I imagined what a life would look like beside Baine, me full of fire and him the wind to keep my flame alive. Two elements. One that sparked the other.

"Will you?" Baine lifted my chin with his finger, staring into my eyes.

"I'm an adult. I think I can manage an eccentric lord." My heart beat loudly in my ears as Baine rested his forehead against mine.

"Do you think I could bear to see another male touch you?"

"You don't own me."

He growled in my ear, forcing me to admit my feelings, however crazy they were. His fingers danced along my skin, causing every part of me to wish we could stay under the moonlight in the woods forever.

A cold wind blew around us, ruffling Baine's silver hair around his face. The stark contrast of his light lavender eyes and dark skin made him appear wild, dangerous, but something in the way he looked at me told me he'd never harm me. Though, I couldn't quite understand why he cared about a wild thing like me, I liked it.

He drummed his fingers against my skin. "Keep your ability hidden and I will find a way to stop his plans and save the prospects. As long as he doesn't choose you, you'll be free. I swear it. I will not let you or any of the other females be sent to war."

"You have to be careful. I don't want you to get in trouble."

The tips of his rough fingers sent sparks across my skin. Bringing his mouth close to my ear, he kissed my cheekbone. "Do not worry about me."

"Easier said than done," I grumbled.

"It's been a long time since I've felt like this," Baine said, taking me in his arms.

"Like what?"

"Alive."

That word sent my heart into a wicked tailspin.

Alive.

That's exactly how I felt right now.

We kissed once more, before breaking apart.

"Okay," I said in a breathy tone. "Now, take me back before we're both discovered."

Baine lifted me, kissing my lips again before flying like the wind through the forest and back into my room before anyone knew we were gone.

Safely inside, I locked my door, and held a finger to my lips.

The moonlight shone in from the window, landing on him as he stood in the center of my room, arms crossed. His shaggy silver hair covered part of his face and I wanted to see all of him.

I took the collar and walked over, holding it against my neck. "You need to put it back on."

With one hand, he swept my hair up and used the other to clasp the collar on and lock it. "You should sleep."

"I don't think I'll be able to. Not after I know the truth." I grabbed his arms for security. "I'm scared. I'm scared for the girls, for you, for myself. I feel helpless right now."

Tomorrow, I'd have to face the other women knowing what fate awaited us all and not be able to tell them. I'd always considered myself strong, but this was a strength I didn't know if I had.

"Come." Baine led me to the bed where he tucked me in under the blankets.

Sitting on the edge of the bed in his tight leathers and hooded cloak, he reminded me of darkness and starlight. He leaned over and brushed the hair off my face. "You are an enigma to me."

Holding the blankets tight, I hung on to his every word. "Why do you say that?"

Still brushing my hair with his finger, he continued, “Aside from Lord Demious and my men, humans have always looked upon me with fear and hatred, but you don’t.”

“Why would I hate you?”

“Because I am fae and people fear what they do not understand.”

I reached out and took his hand closest to me. He tensed then relaxed.

“You have given me no reason to hate you. In fact . . .”

My voice trailed, the flutters in my stomach enlarging to the size of the monarch moths and making me pause. How did I feel about Baine?

“What were you going to say?” There was an eagerness in his tone.

“Well,” I stammered, not knowing how to express what I was feeling. I definitely didn’t want to sound like a fool. “You’ve been kind and gentle, when you’re not bossing me around.”

At that, his lip quirked up.

“You are a very strong-willed woman.” He leaned over and kissed my forehead. “Sleep well, and tomorrow try to hide those flames in your eyes when I walk by.”

“I’ll do my best, though I’m sure it’ll be very trying.” I batted my eyelashes for added effect.

Though we didn’t say it, we both knew when the sun rose, *everything* would change.

NINETEEN

BAINE

The white mare had died during the night. The wound had festered until blackness covered the entire horse. Lord Demious had spent years studying the darkthings: abilities, weaknesses, cures to their wounds. One thing everyone knew, unless the wound was treated with a life crystal, there was no cure, and the crystals were slowly diminishing from Saol. Lord Demious could've attempted to save the horse with one of his life crystals he had hidden away, but they were too precious and had to be used sparingly. The magistrate would not waste such a precious mineral on an animal, though I highly disagreed.

"Still no sign of the darkthing that did this?" I asked.

"None, and we've searched everywhere. There hasn't been another attack since the orchard. It doesn't make sense." Marco washed his hands in the basin. "Something is not right. And what is he planning today? Did you see what he made us capture?"

"I did."

Before dawn, Lord Demious asked part of the guard to leave the estate and catch a moon cat. Beautiful creatures with silver and black fur and large floppy ears. Their cute appearance is a guise as the animals were nasty and quick to attack.

"These tests are ridiculous. He should pick a bride and be done with it." Marco nudged my shoulder. "There they are."

Ms. Begalia led the females out to the staged area on the grounds. Rosalie walked near the back with her exotic friend. Seeing Rosalie made me tense. She should have left, but she was stubborn and difficult. I'd never been more frustrated and conflicted. Staying would risk her life. Going would put Demious on the hunt, but that was something I could deal with, even take control over as long as he didn't suspect me which was a possibility. Very few even knew of the hidden entrance to his laboratory.

Rosalie laughed at something her friend said and looked my way. When our gazes met, she nibbled her bottom lip. It took everything in me to not whisk her off into the woods and take her away from this place. After last night, I realized how much I cared for the human. I shouldn't, yet I couldn't ignore how I came alive in her presence.

Lord Demious would need to choose a bride today, and I would sway him to another female, reminding him he needed a woman of extreme talent. Though the man rarely listened to the advice of others, I had earned his respect and he would listen to me. After that, I would plan a way to free Rosalie on the road to the Borderlands along with the other humans.

The moon cat hissed in the cage. Marco sighed.

"Be on your guard," I said. "If the darkthing is out there, we need to be prepared."

The women gathered outside the training circle. Lord Demious motioned for Marco to bring him the moon cat. Though I sensed her watching me, I could not acknowledge Rosalie in Lord Demious' presence.

"Good morning!" Lord Demious smiled and clasped his hands in front of his chest. "Today will be the last chance for you all to convince me why I should choose you as a bride. Remember, the woman I choose will have her debt fully paid while the others will be forced to work for three years. Do not hold back in this exercise."

The Haalow sisters huddled near each other. The youngest one had red rings around her eyes as if she had been crying for hours. I never did learn how his night with the trio went, but from the distraught looks, not well.

Marco dropped the cage in the circle and stepped out to take point opposite me.

"This is a moon cat," Lord Demious said. "A wild creature who will attack if it feels threatened. As my wife you must be prepared to defend and fight at all times."

The humans whispered to one another; most had probably never been in a fight. I knew Rosalie could protect herself, but the thought of Lord Demious putting her in harm's way sent a wave of fury through me. I gripped the hilts of my swords to contain the rage and remind myself she'd be in more danger if I revealed my feelings.

"Alicia, step forward." Lord Demious motioned the frail girl to him.

Rosalie whispered in Alicia's ear before the terrified thing moved.

Keeping his smile wide, Lord Demious took the human's trembling hands. "Once the barrier is up, I will release your collar and the beast. If

I sense you are unable to protect yourself, I will step in." He gazed out at the remaining females. "Do not fret my beauties, I shall keep you all safe. This is merely a test of strength."

Uneasiness settled in my bones, and by Marco's frown, I sensed he felt it too. I stepped closer and directed the nearby guards to close the circle around the area.

Alicia shook, and if Lord Demious noticed, he didn't act on it. He removed her collar and stepped behind the cage.

"Prepare yourself," he said.

I blinked at the human, unsure if my eyes deceived me, but her body became almost ethereal.

Lord Demious released the moon cat and backed away from the creature with a smirk on his face.

The poor human shrunk back from the creature as it stalked forward, hissing.

This was a ridiculous test. Alicia had no offensive magical ability. What did Lord Demious hope to achieve?

The moon cat launched forward, and Alicia disappeared.

Moving closer, I kept my hands on my weapons, ready for anything.

Lord Demious stared at the spot Alicia had been standing. The cat jumped and pawed before suddenly screeching and running into the cage.

Darkness filled the barrier.

Marco sprinted forward, I followed.

"Lord Demious!" I yelled as I rushed ahead, smashing into the barrier.

"I can't get through," Marco grunted from the other side.

A loud wailing came from inside the barrier. The air in front of me cracked like ice shattering. Readying my swords, I waited for the protection spell to break and release the danger inside.

In a blast of smoke, the barrier broke, sending black mist pouring out into the air around us. Screams from the humans mingled with my own men shouting. I focused on the area in front of me, listening for movement.

I saw the black tentacle before the beast.

Lord Demious had his magical coils wrapped around a darkthing. The massive beast blocked out the sun. I had seen darkthings, but never one so large. Its ethereal form resembled a bull on two legs. Horns curled forward with smoke misting around it.

Its white hollow gaze locked on me.

Lord Demious grunted as he held the monster at bay with his tentacles, but it wasn't enough. I dashed forward, ignoring the scream I knew came from Rosalie, and sliced at the beast in front of me.

My blade went right through the mist.

"You can't use normal attacks," Lord Demious grunted. "Only magic or poison."

My own abilities provided me with speed, not offensive magic spells, but my blades had an energy function.

Marco ran at the flank of the creature, chopping his axe into its side. The axe had a serrated edge dipped in poison. The darkthing howled and the sound pierced my ears, bringing me to my knees.

A blood curdling scream erupted from behind me. I glanced over my shoulder as a winged darkthing targeted the prospects. Somehow, darkthings had emerged from the plane Alicia had entered and now they were here.

Rosalie.

Our gazes met and she clawed at her collar, the fire in her eyes coming to life.

"Lord Demious!" I screamed and dove under the claws of the darkthing in front of me. "Release the prospects. We need the magic."

He grunted and yanked on the tentacles shooting from his hands. "I can't remove them with this in my grasp."

"Release it and I'll keep it busy." Rising to my feet, I swirled my weapons in my hands and pressed the buttons on the hilts, covering the blades with lightning.

"Very well, ready."

I faced the howling monstrosity, bouncing on my heels, eager to tear into the creature in front of me. It had been decades since I fought a creature as deadly as this. "Go."

The moment Lord Demious removed the coils, I launched forward, blades slashing at the ethereal beast. Electricity collided with the darkness, sending waves of lightning crackling through the creature's body. It howled and swung, nearly missing my face as I dodged the massive paw. With my speed, the darkthing could not move fast enough to catch me.

Hit after hit, I stabbed the tips of my swords around its body, creating a whirlwind of lightning arcing through the beast's form. Streaks of blue danced inside the black mist resembling a wild storm, igniting the beast into a frenzy. Dashing behind and in front, I was a whirlwind of death, cycloning around the darkthing, disappearing faster than I appeared.

It roared and spewed a cloud of mist back and forth, catching me in the deadly mist.

Tingles went through my body, my vision blurred.

Sounds muffled in my ears, and I shook my head trying to dislodge the swarm of confusion entering my mind.

The darkthing swatted and connected to my body, suddenly corporeal, and sent me flying onto my back. Landing with a crack, I gazed up at the creature charging forward. Whatever magic it casted, the spell affected my muscles and mind, clouding everything.

Raising my swords, I prepared to block the incoming blow.

Fire tore through the beast's body.

Orange and red blazed around the darkthing as it screeched an earsplitting cry. Taking the moment to move, I rolled to the side out of danger. My breaths came slow, but the sudden cloudiness lifted.

Rosalie stood before the beast who turned its attention to her. Flames sprouted from her hands and her hair rose in waves, riding on the air, her beautiful face taut with focus.

The darkthing decreased in size and flailed at her.

In a blast of heat, the flames consumed her until she was nothing but fire, all-consuming fire that destroyed the beast into ash.

When the darkthing crumbled, the fire receded until Rosalie stood there, naked, and sweating. Our gazes met for a moment before her eyes rolled back.

I had her in my arms before she hit the ground.

Her skin burned mine and I grimaced at the searing pain. Without thinking, I whisked her away into the gardens to the pool.

With her in my arms, burning through my flesh, I stepped into the cool water, letting it wash over the both of us. Sweat covered her rosy skin. Every area burned to touch. I gazed at her bare in my arms, the fear that she might be hurt overpowering the burning on my skin.

"Rosalie," I whispered and carefully dipped her body under, making sure not to cover her face. Steam rose from the surface as her hot body reacted to the water.

She shuddered in my grasp.

Coolness coated my burning skin. Though the flesh had been seared, my natural healing ability slowly knit it back together. Knowing I would be fine, I focused on the delicate human in my arms.

She had risked everything to protect us.

To protect me.

Holding her close, I listened to her heart and lungs which both sounded normal. Though the magic she exuded would drain her for a while, she wasn't hurt.

"Is she okay?" Ara huffed, catching her breath.

"She will be."

Ara brought a long blanket. "I saw what she

did. Lord Demious ordered the girls and guards to handle the minor darkthing, but she ignored them. She walked forward and lit that beast you were fighting on fire."

"She saved my life," I said, replaying the courageous act over and over in my head. Not only did she save me and everyone else, she did it without thought, without realizing what would happen once Lord Demious saw her ability in action.

I lifted Rosalie out of the water and wrapped the blanket around her. "She needs to rest."

"Let's bring her inside."

This time when I brought Rosalie to her room, I didn't run. I held her in my arms, already thinking of a way I could free her from this place. After her display, Lord Demious would choose her as his bride, and it would take every favor I owed to change his mind.

He couldn't marry her.

Not when in my heart, she already belonged to me.

TWENTY

ROSALIE

When I woke, sunlight filtered in through the windows. I remembered fighting that horrid beast, but nothing after. *How did I get here?*

The blanket rubbed against my skin, my very naked skin.

Panic rose in my chest.

"You're finally awake." Lord Demious sat in a chair near the bed, bags under his eyes.

"What happened?" I hugged the blanket to my chest, covering myself. Did Lord Demious bring me here?

"You destroyed a very powerful creature, something I didn't think possible from one of my prospects."

"Is that a good thing or a bad thing?"

He chuckled. "A good thing."

Where was Baine? I couldn't ask about him, but I needed to know if he was hurt. "Is everyone okay. Did anyone get hurt?"

Lord Demious frowned. "One of my guards got attacked. His wounds are grievous, but he'll live."

"I'm sorry." I held in the tears, fearing it was Baine. "And Alicia?"

"Missing."

"How?"

Lord Demious leaned forward and took my hand. "Don't worry about the others. I have good news."

His touch made me want to recoil underneath the blankets. "Oh?"

He smiled wide and my chest heaved with panic.

"After seeing you attack that darkthing, I know you're the one. Congratulations, Rosalie, I choose you."

No, he can't choose me.

"I'll let you rest. We'll announce it at dinner." With that he kissed my hand and left the bedroom.

Once the door closed, I sobbed into the pillow.

Baine had tried to help me escape and I

ignored the chance. Now, he could be the guard hurt, and worse, I would have to marry Lord Demious. The girls would be sent away, and I had to hope Baine would find a way to save them.

I didn't want to marry Lord Demious, not after realizing how much I cared for Baine. The thought made my chest ache with pain and anxiety.

Reaching up to my neck, I sobbed realizing the collar had been fastened back on, keeping me and my magic a slave. I threw the pillow across the room with a scream.

What have I done?

Stupid, idiot.

Pulling at the ends of my hair, I cried out. I wanted to punch something, to let out my anger and frustration that threatened to consume me.

How was I going to marry that vile man? And would he keep this collar on me knowing how powerful I really was? My home, my firehawks . . . and Baine. Would I be forced to be near him every day and not touch him? How could I finally find someone who made me feel alive and have them be torn from my grasp.

My mind frantically thought of Lord Demious and how I would be forced to have his child. When I refused, would he use those black tentacles of his to tie me up and make me submit?

Digging my face into the blankets, I tried to pretend this was all a bad dream.

By the time the twins came to dress me, I had emptied myself of tears.

Ara sat on the edge of my bed while her sister gathered a dress from the wardrobe. "How are you feeling?"

"Lord Demious was here . . . he said . . . he picked me." The words came out in a jumbled mess.

"I'm happy he chose you," Ara said, then lowered herself to my face. "But I know someone who won't be."

Ignoring the shock of her hinting at Baine, I risked asking. "Is he hurt? Demious mentioned a guard."

"Not him. He whisked you away as soon as your magic spent, and you were standing there naked."

"Naked?"

Ara giggled. "All the servants know Baine can move like the wind, but I've never seen him act so quickly."

My heart swelled knowing Baine was safe and he had protected me. "I don't want to marry Lord Demious."

Ara's sister walked over, and we ended the conversation. "I think this is a fitting dress for the announcement, don't you?"

Luna held up a satin rose-hued gown with a sweetheart neckline and beaded bodice, a revealing, but extraordinarily beautiful dress. "You must be so happy."

When Luna walked away, Ara patted my shoulder. "It'll work out. Marrying Lord Demious was why you came here, right?"

I couldn't tell her the truth. I nodded, pretending my entire world wasn't shattering. Not only would I be forced to marry a man I didn't love, but what about Baine? Would I be forced to be near him every day knowing we could never be together?

Numbness replaced the worry as the twins laced and prodded, primping me to perfection. Even though the face in the mirror exuded beauty and confidence, part of me was dying inside.

Did I make a mistake in staying here?

"It's time, miss." Ara placed a gentle hand on my arm. "Everyone is meeting in the dining hall."

Did Baine already know? If only there was more time. I wished I could talk to him, to make a plan. My chest ached, a deep hollow pain encompassing every thought.

When we reached the landing near the grand staircase, Lord Demious stood at the bottom of the stairs, smiling, Baine beside him. Dressed in all black, the sorrowful expression on his face looked as dark and dangerous as his clothes. Did he already talk to Lord Demious?

I grabbed the railing to steady myself, hoping I didn't faint and roll my way down.

"You look magnificent." Lord Demious kissed my hand before looping my arm around his—I didn't miss the fury in Baine's light eyes. "Are you ready to share the good news?"

"Actually, I need a few moments in the washroom. May I meet you inside?"

"Of course." Lord Demious kissed my hand again and I forced a smile out.

I turned, dress gathered in my hands and rushed toward the washroom.

Tears fell as I burst through the door and shut it behind me.

Staring at the mirror on the wall, I cried, forcing myself to think past the sadness and fear.

Moments later, the door swung open, and Baine walked in.

"Baine?"

He locked the door behind him.

Before he could speak, I threw my arms around his neck, crying. "I'm so glad you're safe. I should've listened to you. I'm sorry. What are we going to do?"

His body tensed and though he had his arms around me, he wasn't hugging me back.

"What is it?" I pulled away, searching his eyes for answers.

"There is nothing to do," he said in a deep voice while removing my arms from him. "You will marry Lord Demious."

"What about the girls?"

"I will have their caravan intercepted before it reaches the Borderlands. My promise to you will remain. They will be safe."

I didn't want to ask the next question, but I had to know. "And us?"

"Us?"

The fact he responded with a question made me realize he didn't feel the same as I did. But how could he not? No one kisses with that much passion without caring. He admitted his feelings. Why was he ignoring them now?

"Lord Demious has made his decision, and you are his." Baine spat the words out and avoided looking directly at me. "I warned you, but you refused to listen to me. You could've left this place and now you will be stuck here forever."

"I'm sorry, you said—"

He lifted his hand cutting me off. "What transpired between us is over. This is the last time you and I will speak."

"How can you say that? Was that moment in the woods a lie? Is this a lie?" Pressing my mouth to his, I forced him to remember the promises we made. When he didn't return the kiss, I kissed harder until he caved under my touch and let me in, but that quick reprieve ended as soon as it started.

"No," he growled and pried me off like I burned. Stepping back, he glared at me with such anger I held a hand to my mouth to stifle the sob attempting to break free. "Nothing will change. You are his now."

His words pierced through me, cutting me deeper than they should have. They were full of hurt and rage. Though he acted as if I meant nothing to him, his balled fists shook. I put us in this position, and Baine was making a choice . . . and it wasn't me.

"I understand," I said through the tears. "Though your feelings may have changed, mine haven't. I'm sorry I ruined what could have been the greatest love of our lives."

His eyes widened and for a moment the anguish in his gaze reflected my own. He stared at me, his jaw twitching, his fists shaking, his resolve teetering on the precipice of death. I wanted to reach out, touch his face, hold him, especially if it was the last time.

I stood on my tip toes and held his face within my hands. He tensed, freezing, and eyeing me with a pained expression.

"Thank you for saving me," I said, my voice cracking as more tears fell. "I made a mistake and now we'll both pay for it."

He trembled beneath my touch, and I kissed him. His mouth stayed in a hard line, almost as if giving in would end us both, and deep down I knew it would.

Before I lost my courage, I rushed out of the washroom and into the hall. No one waited for me, and the emptiness matched the hollow ache inside my chest. Balling my fists, I tried to rein in my emotions. I didn't want anyone to see me like this.

The door to the washroom opened and shut. I didn't need to turn around to know who stood behind me. Instead of walking past, footsteps sounded in the opposite direction. It wasn't until those steps disappeared that I finally moved.

Wiping my face with my fingers, I took a few steadying breaths then entered the dining hall.

An empty seat sat next to Lord Demious who at once stood when I entered, holding a goblet. "And there is the woman of the hour, my betrothed, Rosalie."

Sniffles surrounded the table, except Janetta who clapped and seemed genuinely happy. I nodded at the women around me before finding a seat.

Lord Demious had a servant pour me a

goblet of plum wine, which I happily drank, then another. Baine entered the room and took flank near the back corner. Did he notice how Lord Demious slid his hand to my thigh under the table? Did Baine care? Did he purposely keep his distance because anything else was too difficult?

Janetta sat too far for us to speak privately. She glanced my way with a sad look. I gave her a weak smile and drank another goblet of wine. The liquid numbed the pain, but I knew soon I would break, and I didn't think anything would be able to put me back together.

"May I be excused?" I said to Lord Demious.

He frowned. "Are you ill?"

"This is a lot, and I still haven't recovered from the fight."

"Of course, my dear." Lord Demious stood and took my hand. "Excuse us. My betrothed is a bit spent. Enjoy your meal, ladies."

With his clammy hand on my arm, he pulled me alongside him. I glanced at Baine, hoping to see something in those lavender eyes, instead he purposefully looked away.

Outside in the corridor, Lord Demious patted my arm. "You need to relax. I will take you to my private quarters where you will not be disturbed."

I wasn't ready to be anywhere private with

this lord. We passed by the open library. "Will you show me your history collection? If I'm to rule, I'd like to learn more about Farrow's Gate."

He smiled wide, seeming pleased with my request. "I knew I chose correctly."

If I could keep Lord Demious at bay, I might be able to find a way out of this disastrous situation. His touch made me squirm with uneasiness like stepping on a slug with bare feet. Slugs weren't so awful from a distance, but up close they were slimy and gross.

We entered the library, and the sight made my heart swell, slightly lifting the heaviness in my chest. Father had tomes at home, but nothing of this size. Sunlight streamed through the stained-glass windows, creating rainbows along the bookshelves. While the library in the host tower had more books, it held none of the beauty here.

"There are many stories within these walls, and you will have access to all of them." Lord Demious leaned into me as he spoke, his breath smelling of onion soup.

I turned my head, swaying a bit from all the wine, sweat beading my hairline. Heat stuffed the air, making the room oppressive and sweltering. Lord Demious sauntered behind me, placing his hands on my waist.

"You are very beautiful." He slid his hands

along my bodice, and I held back the urge to slap him.

I'd find a way out of here, but not with fighting him. "Thank you, my lord."

"You saved us yesterday," he whispered, pulling me closer. "You were magnificent. I never expected your fire magic to be so powerful. You and I will create a lineage unlike any before."

Each praise made my skin crawl with disgust.

"I can't wait until we wed tomorrow." His body pressed against me, and I was glad he was behind me, unable to see the disgust on my face.

"Tomorrow?" My voice quaked and he gripped my waist tighter.

"I don't see the need to wait . . . for anything." He pulled my hair aside and kissed my neck.

I wanted to scream. "I'm very tired. I should retire."

Ignoring my request, he lifted my dress.

"Lord Demious, please." Tears pricked my eyes.

"Shh," he said, pressing me against the nearby table. "We will be husband and wife, and as your betrothed it's my duty to make sure you are satisfied. I know how to please a woman. I promise to ease away all that worry and fear."

"Then you will allow me to retire."

"You will, soon."

Disgust filled my mouth and I wanted to

vomit. Quickly, I thought of what I should do to remove myself from this situation, but my heart was heavy. This is what Baine tried to rescue me from.

Cold fingers tugged at the front of my dress near the neckline.

"My lord." I placed my hand on his, holding back the urge to dig my nails into his skin and rip him to shreds. "I have never been with a man, and I would like my first time to be a bit more, romantic."

"I assumed a woman of your age had at least dabbled."

"Can we wait for our wedding night? Please?"

"I am not a cruel man," he whispered, sliding his hand under my dress. "Do not fear me. I know my actions the night of the ball were a bit harsh, but you will understand my purpose here and yours, soon enough."

Sweet words, yet he continued to rub against my skin.

"A kind man would honor the wishes of his betrothed."

"Lord Demious," Baine yelled from somewhere behind us.

"You better have a good explanation for interrupting me," Lord Demious snarled, but made no move to remove his hands which had moved up to my bodice. "I am not to be disturbed when I am with my bride."

"The agent has returned, again, this time with men."

"Sorry, my dear." He turned me around and smiled. "I must go, but I promise that tomorrow night when I bed you, it will be more than romantic."

With a clammy kiss to my cheek, he bid me farewell.

Baine's jaw twitched and he gripped his sword hilts so tight, the skin on his knuckles lightened.

Lord Demious left the room, Baine's glare meeting mine, before he slammed the door shut.

TWENTY-ONE

BAINE

Lord Demious frowned as we walked outside to meet the Borderlands Agent. The sight of Demious' hands on Rosalie plagued my mind, but I had to ignore the festering anger and deal with the visitors on the lawn.

"I thought we had an understanding?" Demious clasped his hands in front of his robes.

Marco and three of my men flanked the agents, waiting for my signal. If the agents tried to discuss the situation with violence, they would find our blades in their necks.

"The situation has changed." The agent took out a rod and I grabbed the hilts of my swords. Sensing our unease, the agent held up a hand to make us pause. "Easy. Someone wishes to speak to you."

With the black rod in his hand, the agent swirled it in a circle, creating a blue glowing light. The portal opened and a young woman with stark blonde hair, dressed in a white and red high collared dress, stepped out.

"Kelia?" Lord Demious moved forward.

"Hello, Demious."

"It's been a long time." Demious waved at me to stand down. "You look well."

Demious had many friends in high places, but I never remembered him talking about the Magi Council with any type of reverie. Whoever this woman was, she was important, and powerful.

"And you look old." She walked past him, ignoring the flicker of awe in Demious' eyes. "Bring the girls to me. I will test them now."

"I've already made my choice." Demious scampered after the blonde woman. "You can have the rest."

I flinched at the mention of his future bride. Rosalie would be nothing more than a child bearer for him. He showed more admiration to this stranger than the woman he was supposed to marry.

"We don't have time for your games. Bring all the girls to me."

"Of course, Kelia." Demious snapped his

fingers at me. "Gather the girls from the dining hall and bring them here."

"Understood." Giving a bow, I turned on my heel, thankful that Demious' selfish nature would keep Rosalie out of this exercise. She was the only one not in the hall, and after how I left, she would most likely be in her room or somewhere else.

Marco stepped next to me as we entered the mansion. "What's going on? Why is Kelia here?"

"You know her?"

"You don't?" Marco spoke in hushed tones. "Don't let her age fool you. That's Kelia Ironstone. One of the magi's strongest mages, and she does whatever they say, without question or sympathy."

"It doesn't matter. Bring the girls out to her. I'll meet you there."

"Where are you going?"

"I need to check on something."

Shaking his head, Marco took the other guards and headed down the corridor.

Using my swiftness, I flashed to the library. I needed to make sure Rosalie was still there. There was no question that she was the strongest woman here. Even if the magistrate had chosen his bride, the magi woman couldn't be trusted. The only way to ensure Rosalie's safety was to keep her far away from the agents.

I opened the door to an empty room.

Where did she go?

"Rosalie?"

Stepping inside the quiet library, I searched the area, hoping to see a flash of red hair. The air in the room chilled. The unnatural shift sent a warning through my body. Unsheathing my swords, I activated my tattoo. The ivy glowed and with my arm outstretched, I searched for the source.

Nothing, though my fae senses knew better. Something was here.

Slowly backing to the door, I kept my keen gaze focused on the icy atmosphere until I was certain nothing lurked nearby. Pivoting, the moment I exited, I dashed to the dining hall to find the girls had already been escorted out.

Large windows covered the right side of the room. Peeking outside, I looked at the girls being lined up.

And right at the end, next to Janetta, stood Rosalie.

By the time I got outside, I lost all pretense and moved to go straight to her. Lord Demious blocked me before I could come close. He eyed me and I knew in that steady gaze of his, he would handle the situation. Lord Demious was many things, but he was not to be undermined. The magi would never challenge him in fear of what would happen to Farrow's Gate, and that truth gave Lord Demious plenty of power.

Stepping around to flank his side, I watched Rosalie. Even with her eyes red from crying, she held her chin high and met Kelia's inspecting gaze with ferocity and courage.

My instincts wanted to shift and rip the head of the human who threatened my female but fighting would cause more damage than good. I'd wait until Lord Demious gave the word.

Kelia clasped her hands behind her back, walking back and forth in front of the girls. "Lord Demious has not told you everything about this competition of his, but I will."

Whispers exchanged between the prospects and Rosalie balled her fists.

"You are needed for war." Kelia's statement sent gasps and cries through the girls.

Saol only had one war, against the very creatures we fought only a day ago.

"Give me the key to their collars." Kelia held out her hand, never once actually acknowledging Lord Demious.

"I can temporarily dispel—"

"The key, Demious, now." Kelia's voice rose, and a blue energy began emanating from her hand.

He handed it over with a grunt. "I thought we were on the same side."

"We are."

Kelia took the key and stood in front of Janetta. "What can you do? And do not lie. Lying to the magi is treason."

Janetta's lip trembled. Rosalie grabbed her friend's hand and nodded for Janetta to speak.

"Poison," she stammered. "I can spew poison."

"Gas or liquid?"

"Gas."

Kelia nodded, seeming to approve. "That will be helpful in the war. We'll be able to use you."

Janetta cried and Rosalie wrapped an arm around her shoulder, hugging her tight.

When Kelia moved to stand in front of Rosalie, it took all my willpower to not step in front of her and stop whatever Kelia planned on doing. The only thing keeping my swords at bay was Lord Demious. His selfishness would not allow his bride to be taken, regardless of who gave the order.

"You," Kelia said. "What can you do?"

"That one is not for the Council." Lord Demious moved Janetta aside and slid his arm around Rosalie's waist. "You should be resting."

With a wide smile, Demious placed his hand on Rosalie's belly. "Kelia, this is my betrothed and she's with child."

Silence followed, and being a quick thinker

Rosalie smiled back, pretending to play along. Though everyone here knew that none of the prospects were here long enough to make that lie even a possibility.

"Baine, escort my betrothed back to her chambers." Lord Demious guided Rosalie to me.

With a relieved sigh I couldn't express, I nodded.

Lord Demious craved power, but he never crossed the magi. To outright lie like this meant he would not play along with whatever agreement he had made. Though I could not be more grateful. When Rosalie came within a foot of me, I placed my hand on her elbow, desperate to touch her skin and know she was safe.

"He's lying!"

Claudia pointed at Demious with fury in her dark eyes.

Kelia narrowed her gaze at Demious.

He smiled. "Old flame, and a bit bitter she wasn't chosen."

"I'm not. Rosalie is a fire mage and the strongest one here. She took an enormous darkthing down by herself."

I tensed, keeping my hand on Rosalie's arm. She glanced up at me, worry filling her eyes.

Kelia looked at Rosalie then back at her guards. "Take her."

No.

Borderlands Agents circled me, and I shoved Rosalie behind my back.

The portal re-opened. “Pay Demious what he’s owed. He can send the rest of the girls in the morning. We’ll take that one now. The magi will want to examine her.” Kelia stepped through, disappearing to the other side.

Dark clouds rolled in overhead, the beginning of another storm. The temperature dropped a few degrees, and wind blew across the grounds.

“It’s okay,” Rosalie whispered behind me, her hand resting on my back. “Let me go.”

“No,” I growled.

I glanced at Lord Demious waiting for him to command me, say something. I owed him a life debt and had been loyal since the moment he saved me, but I couldn’t let them take Rosalie away. I *wouldn’t.*

Understanding dawned in Demious’ eyes and he gave me the tiniest nod.

War it is.

And then I shifted.

TWENTY-TWO

ROSALIE

Baine shifted in front of me, his twin swords falling to the grass. The agents stalked him, and he growled, a menacing sound that sent me stepping back. I snatched one of his swords off the ground, ready to defend myself.

With the collar keeping my flame in the dark, I'd be useless without a weapon. I may not have been a swordsman, but I'd slaughtered enough beasts in the North to know how to protect myself.

Black tentacles wrapped around one of the agent's neck, sweeping him off his feet. He screamed, and Lord Demious slammed him to the ground with a resonating crack. The magistrate's eyes blackened and the smoke pouring from his hands created a cone of death. One of the agents pulled out a rod and waved it in a circle, creating a portal, but Lord Demious snatched the rod out of his hand and shattered it on the ground.

Rain poured from the sky and the thunder drowned out the sound of battle. A bolt of lightning hit a tree in the distance, slicing it in two and sending a shiver of fear through me.

"Set us free!" Janetta yelled, glancing back at me with frightened eyes.

Baine leaped onto one of the agents, biting his neck and crushing the man's windpipe between his powerful jaw. I held the sword with both hands, gripping the hilt tightly, and stepping back away from the carnage.

I wiped the water off my face, blinking through the storm to see what was happening. The remaining guards fought with the Borderlands Agents who released a torrent of magic from their wands. My gaze flitted to the other girls who were separated from me now.

"Run!" I yelled at them. "Go and I'll find the key."

Janetta grabbed two girls and took off toward the stables while the Haalow sisters ran toward the gardens. Kelia had asked for the key, but I could've sworn she tossed it before stepping through the portal. If I could somehow find it . . .

Baine flew across the grass, pouncing on

another agent who screamed as the wolf tore out his throat in one vicious bite. Blood splattered across the ground, soaking Baine's coat. With a flick of his head, he tossed the flesh in his mouth to the grass. I blinked at the awful sight, trying to remember these men were trying to take us into war and they deserved their gruesome fate.

Still, the gory sight turned my stomach.

Sword in hand, I ran alongside the outskirts of the fighting, searching the blood-smeared ground for that key. I slipped, falling onto the grass, and dropping the sword. Baine growled, causing me to turn. He eyed me and shook his head, almost as if he was telling me to run.

"Watch out!" I screamed at him.

His momentary distraction caused one of the agents to sneak up behind him and blast him with a charge from a wand. Baine howled and fell on his back.

"Baine!"

Someone grabbed me from behind in a headlock, quickly covering my mouth with their hand. I'd been so distracted on the scene in front of me, I didn't think to check behind me. I kicked across the ground as the man kept his arm around my throat, dragging me away from the battle.

I tried to yell, but only gurgled a helpless plea. Digging my nails into my attacker's skin,

I kicked and clawed at the person holding me, begging Baine to notice what was happening to me.

"Open the portal," the man holding me said.

Glancing back, another agent stood by the trees. They'd pulled me around the corner of the mansion, blocked from where everyone else fought.

No. No.

My flame flickered, fighting to break free of the magical darkness the collar had stuffed it in, but no matter how hard I tried, no matter how deep I searched, the fire inside me wasn't strong enough to overpower the dampener.

No one saw me disappear. I'd be dragged away to war, never saying goodbye, never seeing my home again. Never seeing Baine . . .

White dots blinked in and out of my vision as the agent dragged me across the hard ground, closer to the swirling circle of magic leading to a place of death and darkness. My body flipped over, hitting my chin on a rock, shooting pain through my jaw. The Borderlands shimmered through the portal; a tattered outpost under siege, surrounded by a barren area coated in a sandy beige blanket that sent a wave of panic through my body.

"Hurry," one of the agents said, waving at his companion to move faster.

I slapped, hit, kicked, anything to give me a chance to dislodge myself.

The agent dragging me removed his hand and punched me in the face, causing my mind to haze and the fight in me to momentarily leave my body. He yanked me off the ground, lifted me into his arms and ran toward the portal, his companion going in first.

At the last moment, lightning zipped behind me, separating me from the agent. I cried and fell sideways, rolling out of the way and back into Farrow's Gate.

Baine, still in his wolf form, and glowing in blue light, tore at the agent who held me only a moment ago, shredding the man to pieces as they both disappeared into the portal.

A massive shadow beast bit the head off the first agent who went through the portal. His comrade had just enough time to scream before the clawed hand of a darkthing swatted him fifty feet into the air. With a quick glance behind me, I could tell the way home had closed.

Wails and screams echoed around me. The sounds of the dying clashed with the hungry cries of the darkthings swarming the camp. Blackened shadows of death converged on their prey as I stood alone in the center of this flesh banquet. Still in my wolf form, I vaulted off the muddy ground and at a creature whose maw was bigger than my head. The electric surrounding my fur in a chaotic cocoon arced around the beast as I tore into its sinewy flesh, ripping it into shreds.

Someone's bloody limb flew past me, another soldier minced into a bloody mist as the shadow creatures eviscerated what little resistance was left, decimating soldiers as they ran franticly over the sea of dead. I didn't know where I had landed, but one look at the horizon told me enough. Even though the Rift was still miles away, its maleficent eye pulsed with shadowy cumulous far in the distance.

I was now in the Borderlands, and from the frenzy surrounding this outpost, it was being overrun.

Activating my speed, I zipped from one beast to the next, letting my magic sizzle, electrocuting anything in the vicinity, but it wouldn't be enough. There were no more men, nothing left but the broken remains of those who had fought and lost. Fear pushed me forward, forcing my rage to control my movements without thought. My anger was the only defense against the despair washing over my thoughts. Terrified at the fact that with no way home, Rosalie would meet a similar fate.

This is what Lord Demious had planned for the females? This was the certain demise he would send them off to.

If I survived this onslaught, he would answer for this bloodshed. I could no longer serve such a depraved man.

With nothing left alive, the darkthings converged on me, too many to differentiate. Using my speed and magic, I leapt around franticly, biting and clawing my way through the roving tides of decimation, never staying in one section too long. My only chance of surviving this encounter would be to run out of the battle and toward the base camp which would be miles in the other direction. However, I was deep behind the enemy lines as this forward camp was no longer a bastion of safety.

A flash of red and orange erupted on the back of a monstrosity to my left, boring a hole which sizzled through its chest. To my surprise, a figure wreathed in flames, slowly walked forward, fire leaping from the inferno engulfing him, igniting everything in the area. Jumping back before I was caught in that deadly stream, I watched the man sweep a torrent of flame from his outstretched hands, incinerating a score of the vile aberrations that were converging on my flank.

Using the distraction, I continued my own fight, zipping around the blaze and tearing through the dark ones who got too close. Slick with vital fluid, human and abomination alike, the ground was saturated in its mixture, forming a black ichor. My paws slid across the tainted ground which had been fused into glass, the raging furnace beside me had melted the sand into a smooth surface. The blood shed made the grounds extremely slippery, but I stayed in the fight sliding wildly as I fought alongside this flaming creature. A beast with no eye and only a round hole with teeth slammed on top of me, snapping at my face.

My reserves were low, but I had enough magic left in me for one more jolt. Electric current crackled from out of my fur, the voltage electrocuting the monster on top of me. It howled, collapsing upon me. Struggling beneath its oppressive weight I strained to crawl out from under its dead body. Panting and pinned, I focused on the remaining darkthings, who were converging in a swarm of death. Changing back into fae form would be risky without my swords which were back in Farrow's Gate. I'd have to keep fighting. Wriggling wildly, I fought to free myself from the overbearing mass. It was too late as the horde of slaughter dove at me, fangs dripping with hunger.

Heat slammed into my back and my yelp mingled with a thousand cries as the air shimmered orange and red. A nebulous of flame roared loudly, engulfing those cries silencing them forever.

Darkness swallowed me and I thought I was dead, but the smell of my own burnt hide assured me that this wasn't the case. Shaking franticly, the pile of ash encasing me dissipated into the desert breeze. Soot covered and singed, the body which had trapped me in a certain death, had become my shelter. Its wispy remains floated off the last bit of static energy that danced on my chard fur.

Turning around, a naked man sat on his knees, head hanging low, smoke wafting off his skin. He lifted his head, smiling like a mad man. His wild red hair reminded me of another human who wielded fire.

"Well, hello there, pup. How did you get here?"

I growled at the word pup, and he chuckled. "Okay, wolf, my mistake."

He sighed and stood, black ichor covering most of his skin. "I need to get back to base camp and tell them what happened before more of those things come. I used the last of my magic taking care of this little incursion."

The man bent over, and I turned my head, not needing to see a full few of his backside. Through the years, I'd learned that humans tended to speak freely around animals, always expecting them to be just what they appeared. Unlike the fae who would never say anything incriminating in front of a fly for fear it was a spy or worse.

A thump made me turn around. The stranger lay on his side, either passed out or dead. He had managed to steal a pair of pants off a soldier before falling to the ground. Nudging his shoulder with my nose, I attempted to wake the man. I could have left him to his fate, but besides the fact he reminded me too much of another human, he had just saved my life.

More forceful, I shoved my head under his arm, forcing him to his feet.

He grabbed my fur, and I shimmied my body under his chest until he shifted and climbed on to my back. If he could hold on, I could get us out of here.

"Run fast and straight," he whispered, gripping my sides. "Another minute and we'll be swarmed."

Glancing back, a shadow moved across the horizon. A swirling mass too far away to discern. The Rift in the Never created an everlasting portal from the shadow realm to here. Every living being with ill intent ended up in the Shadow Realm. A place of never-ending torment where souls perished for eternity and twisted into madness and darkthings. The malice of that place encroached on us now and I would not fall to its murderous grip.

Sprinting, I made haste for the base camp. My newfound companion held on, though as I ran over corpses, his grip on me lessened. The cloudy hazed sky made it difficult to see the sun, but I knew in hours this place would be covered in night with a darkness to match the Rift. There was no way to know how far I'd need to run to get us back to camp or worse, if the magi would even let me enter.

Tents scattered the forward camp, trampled and some burning from magic or thrown torches. The entire camp had been decimated, nothing lived, not even the monsters who had attacked this area. What happened here? How did the darkthings converge on the magi's camp and win? Lord Demious had mentioned the magi were close to a spell that would close the Rift for good. Could the creatures in the Never sense that?

A mass of shadows writhed in the distance ahead of us. The acrid smell of death permeated the air. Going forward to the base camp was no longer an option. I'd have to veer left or right and stay far from that unknown horde.

I'd never been to this area of Saol and knew little about the Borderlands. Glancing up at the sky, I searched for the sun, hoping its position would give me the right direction to head in.

The hazed sky told me nothing. Sniffing the air, I searched the winds for any scent other than death. In my wolf form, I could smell for around two miles. The air to the west had a slighter better air quality. I couldn't decipher anything specific other than a tinge of cleanliness.

An unnatural howl emitted from the mass converging ahead. The time for decisions was over and I sprinted to the west, following my senses to a safer area. The human on my back didn't stir as I ran, the growing darkness fading into the distance. Even with my magic, I wouldn't be able to run far, and I would have no energy to fight any threat that might come upon us.

My muscles strained against the weight of the human on my back as the run took all that I had. Day switched to night and the hazed sky darkened. Shadows of gray past us in the night and I shook the dizziness from my head, knowing I was almost at my limit. A salty breeze wafted in my nose, and I pushed myself harder, faster, eager to reach the cleaner air. The barren grounds shifted, turning from areas of dead wood to soft patches of grass and thin trees that filled the area and birthed a new woodland with foxtail that swayed with the wind.

My paws sunk into the sand as I crested a hill and was greeted by the vicious waves of the

Aegis Sea. Slowing to a trot, I found an area on the sand near a large broken piece of driftwood. Lowering myself to my belly, I shimmied back and forth until the sleeping human rolled onto the sand. Nudging his shoulder with my head, I rolled him onto his back.

Far from the Rift and safe for now, I laid on the soft ground. The waves crashed against the shore, the sound soothing and oddly comforting. The man beside me snored, and somewhere between his wheezing and the melody of the sea, I closed my eyes and drifted off.

TWENTY-FOUR

ROSALIE

"Baine!" The magical portal winked out, taking my fae with it.

He had saved me and sent himself to death instead. My hands shook and I screamed, angry, afraid, and helpless. I had to get this wretched collar off my neck. Lord Demious had handed Kelia the key, but she had tossed it on the ground before going through the portal.

Scrambling to my feet, I ran to the side of the mansion, peeking around the corner. Shadows covered Lord Demious from head to toe and shot out at Kelia who must've returned when she realized I wasn't there.

"You will be thrown into the magi prison for

this," she growled and shot out a beam of blue light that pushed against the shadows.

"No, this is my land and I alone control it. You don't have the authority!" The shadows slammed into Kelia, pushing her back.

With a pensive expression, she pulled back her arm and clapped her hands together then pushed out. The force of energy shot a hole through the shadows, sending Lord Demious sliding across the grass. He grimaced but immediately ran forward, and tackled Kelia. She screamed, thrown off guard, and I used that chance to run out and search for the key.

Hiding behind a tree, I watched the two tumble on the soil, a mass of black and blue swirling together in a tornado. Borderlands Agents fought against Lord Demious' guards, making it impossible to move from my spot. How was I supposed to search for a little key with all that fighting?

A hand covered my mouth and I screamed, the sound muffled.

"Shh, it's me," Janetta said.

Before I could speak, the lock on my collar clicked open.

Turning around, I wrapped my arms around her, feeling the pulse of my fire warming my core. "You came back."

"You wouldn't leave me," she whispered and

hugged me back. “I watched where the key fell and grabbed it as soon as I could.”

She took my hand and pulled me back toward the side of the mansion.

“Where are we going?” I watched the fighting, wondering how we were going to escape. “Where is everyone else?”

“Scattered or inside the mansion. Come on. We need to go hide until the fighting stops.” Pulling me through a side entrance, she dragged me into Lord Demious’ home, my mind whirring.

“Here.” Janetta opened the door to the library and slammed it closed behind us. “We can go hide on the upper floor and wait it out.”

“Wait.” I had to stop and think. “We have to leave. We can’t stay here and hide.”

Janetta chewed her bottom lip and her gaze darted from me to the door. “I’m not a fighter.”

Taking her hands, I stared into her frightful gaze. “But I am.”

She shook her head, eyes brimming with tears. “I don’t want to go to war.”

“Would you rather die fighting for a chance of freedom or under the swarm of a thousand monsters?”

With a shaky breath, she squeezed my hands. “Freedom.”

A cold breeze entered the library, making

me turn to the windows which were closed. Instinctively, I tugged Janetta behind me.

"What is it?" she whispered, putting a hand on my back.

"I don't know. Do you—"

My words died in my throat as a black oval appeared in front of us, the air shimmering and stretching. Alicia stepped through the strange portal, her complexion whiter than the last time we saw her.

"Is it true?" Alicia asked.

"Is what true?" Janetta said as she moved to stand behind me. "Where have you been. Are you okay?"

"He's sending the girls to the Borderlands?" Alicia's form seemed ethereal, not fully here.

"Um," I paused, looking at Janetta, confused. Did she sense what I did? "Yes."

Alicia's skin morphed into a ghostly white.

"Alicia? What's happening to you?" Janetta went to step forward, her hand outstretched. Instantly, I blocked her path with my body, shaking my head no.

"My mother was right. She told me he'd been sending women off to war . . . including my sister. Everything that's happened in the south is because of his magic. The plagues, the dead crops. He steals magic to feed his own."

My hands shook. "Wait . . . are you saying

Lord Demious is causing the plagues?"

Alicia nodded. "Many have died at his hands. I needed to be sure."

"My parents . . ." The ache of their loss tore open like an old wound. "They had gone into the southern swamps to find the source of the plague snakes. They never came back."

Janetta grabbed my hand and Alicia's. "Let's leave, together. We can go to my home. We'll be safe there."

Ignoring Janetta, I looked over at Alicia whose gaze shifted black, and I knew we weren't going anywhere. "No."

Fire pulsed through my veins, and I headed for the door. Everything that had gone wrong started with those plague snakes: my parents dying, the firehawks being sick, Calvin going off to war.

"Rosalie, no!" Janetta chased after me, Alicia now by my side. "He's too powerful. You'll both be killed!"

"No, we won't," I said, my flame fueling my steps. I didn't care about hiding anymore. I'd use my full potential, more than when I fought the darkthing. I'd show Lord Demious what an elemental could really do.

Shouts and the clang of metal entered the foyer. The three of us stopped, just around the corner by the side entrance where Janetta and I first came in. A tiny part of me wanted to heed her warning and run away, far from this place, but I couldn't, not when I knew the truth.

When the shouts from inside sounded farther away, we ran across the marble floor to the door. I opened it, and peeked outside, before waving the other two to follow. Heart racing, my head spinning with fear and anger, I cautiously crept to the side of the mansion to see if Kelia and Lord Demious still fought.

Lord Demious straddled Kelia, his hands around her throat and his shadows seeping up into her nostrils and open mouth. His eyes were completely blackened, and wisps of obsidian smoke lifted from his skin. Kelia's right hand glowed blue and she pressed it against his robe, the material disintegrating under her touch, but even when her hand connected with his skin, he didn't budge.

"It's a shame," he hissed, his voice scratchy and deeper than normal. "You and I could've been a powerful union, and I had hoped you would have reconsidered my proposal."

Kelia choked, and he leaned down to her mouth.

"I might even ignore this slight, if you agree to be mine, magic and body." He placed his mouth just above hers as a stream of black spewed from his mouth into hers right before he kissed her, groaning in a wicked display of pleasure.

Her nails dug into his flesh, the glowing flame flickering.

I watched in horror, frozen by his sickening behavior.

"I'm not waiting any longer." Alicia looked at me before the shadow portal that brought her into the library appeared and she stepped inside it, disappearing in a flash.

A scream brought my attention to Lord Demious who was now on his back, writhing on the grass. A trio of wounded Borderlands Agents stood around him, two pointing electric wands at him, the third picked up Kelia into his arms and opened a portal. Once the agent with Kelia stepped through, the other two followed, leaving the estate before Lord Demious could react.

Alicia appeared behind him, a sword in her hand. Somehow, she had picked up a sword from somewhere and now was going to end Lord Demious.

A black tentacle shot out of Lord Demious' hand and curled around Alicia's neck. He picked her up over his head and slammed her onto the grass with a sickening *crack*, the sword slipping from her hand.

"Well, well, if it isn't my missing prospect." He picked up the weapon she had dropped. "I should've killed you the moment I learned you were a shadow walker. After all, your kind are very rare."

"He's going to kill her," Janetta hissed behind me.

I ran out from the tree and sprinted to where they were. "Stop!"

Lord Demious shot an angry glare my way. One hand pressed against the wound on his stomach, the other held the sword tip to Alicia's throat. "You should be thankful. I tried saving you."

"Don't do this. You've already caused enough pain."

"Me?" He laughed.

With the Borderlands Agents dead or gone, the remaining guards began circling us, including Baine's head guard. The dark skinned fae eyed me and Lord Demious, weapon drawn, but making no move in either direction.

"You killed my sister, and you're stealing the life force from the south. Our people are dying because of your plague!" Alicia screamed, tugging at the black tentacle holding her in place.

Thunder boomed and I prayed that rain didn't follow.

Lord Demious laughed, the sound wicked and booming. "You have no proof of such ridiculous claims."

What if Alicia was wrong? I didn't really

think about what she said. I'd been so upset, any common sense disappeared with the idea he could've been the reason my parents died.

But the shy, silent girl we had known didn't stop her accusations. "I've followed you around your home at night, in the shadows, when you think no one is listening. If I show the guards where you keep your poison totems that would be all the proof needed."

"Is that true?" One of the guards stepped forward, blood dripping from a wound on his head. "I have family near the plagued south."

"Lies!" Lord Demious screamed. He lifted the sword and shoved the blade into Alicia's neck.

With a vengeful roar, I shot fire out of my hands, blasting Lord Demious. He quickly pivoted, throwing up a wall of shadow, stopping the fire from reaching him. He growled and shoved the shadows at me, but my fire burned hotter, an endless stream of flames that began to cover my arms and burn the sleeves off my dress.

Sweat dripped from Lord Demious' forehead. "Kill her!"

The guards made no move forward, all seeming to wait for the head guard's direction. Marco held up a hand, stopping them.

"Marco!" Lord Demious yelled as our magic blasted against one another.

"If you can't kill this human then you're

not powerful enough to be the magistrate of Farrow's Gate," the fae replied with a stern expression.

"Fine," Lord Demious growled. "Seems I need to prove my worth."

Black shadows reached around my fire, too many directions for me to concentrate on. The ground beneath me shook as the grass wilted and black smoke wafted into the air to converge with the shadows surrounding me. Shifting my hands, I tried to create a ball around myself, going on the defensive, but as the ground rumbled and the sky boomed with thunder, Lord Demious' magic seeped through my defenses.

Fear pumped through me, the realization everything Alicia said had been true.

He had killed my parents.

And now he was going to kill me.

Smoke snaked up my nose like that night in the garden. Tears filled my eyes as pictures of my family and Baine flickered through my mind. With trembling hands, I fought to push the smoke away, to be more powerful than him. I coughed on the dark magic as it slithered down my throat, trying to destroy me from the inside.

Lord Demious came nearer, his complexion slithering with shadows. "It'll be a shame to kill a creature like you."

His mouth opened wide, a stream of dark magic pouring out and coming closer. I threw a punch, and he grabbed my arm, my flames dissolving under his shadows. With his other hand, he clutched my neck, holding me in place as he moved to put his mouth on mine.

Suddenly, he stopped. His eyes shifting back to his normal brown, a shocked expression dawning on his face.

"Baine may be loyal, but I'm not," Marco snarled from behind Lord Demious as he shoved a sword through the magistrate's chest.

Blood trickled from Lord Demious' mouth and when Marco yanked his sword back out, the magistrate fell over. I stepped back, heaving, confused, tired, dizzy.

I swayed on my feet as white spots blinked in my vision.

"Whoa." Marco slid an arm around my waist. "I've got you. You're safe."

"Did you . . . is he?"

Marco smiled. "I did and yes. I never really liked him."

Relieved, I relaxed into Marcos' embrace, and he scooped me into his arms and off the ground.

"You can rest now. I may not have been loyal to Lord Demious, but I am to Baine. You and the prospects are safe. I swear it. My men and

I will protect you and get you all back home where you belong."

Safe.

For the first time since my brother left, I actually believed it.

TWENTY-FIVE

BAINE

The crackling of a fire woke me. Opening my eyes, I realized I had fallen asleep in my wolf form, something that had not happened since I was a youngling. The human I had carried sat across from me on the sand, nibbling on a crab leg.

“You’re awake,” he said and tossed a crab over. “Figured you’d might be hungry.”

I sniffed at the dead crustacean before my hunger took over and I bit into the shell, crushing it between my fangs.

“There’s a good pup. Knew you’d like that.”

I growled at the word pup, and he laughed.

“Sorry. How about I call you wolfie? I need to call you something.”

The smirk on his face reminded me of another human. The similarities too close to be a coincidence. Between the red hair, the slender nose, and wild blue eyes, I felt like I was staring at a male version of Rosalie.

Could they be related? I needed to know.

The human sighed. “Well, you got us to safety, and I thank you for that. We’re too far from the base camp, but we are closer to my home.” His gaze lifted to the sky, and he smiled. “I think you may have just given me my freedom. They’ll never know I survived, and I can go home. Oh, is Rosy going to be pissed at me for being gone so long. Wait until you meet my sister. She’s going to love you.”

At the mention of a sibling, I shifted, all pretensions gone.

His eyes widened and he froze mid-bite, the crab leg an inch away from his mouth. “That’s a neat party trick.”

“Is your sister Rosalie Hawk?”

Flames ignited in his eyes, all playfulness gone. “How do you know my sister?”

“I don’t have time to explain. She’s in danger and we need to head to Farrow’s Gate.” I stood, stretching out my limbs and cracking my neck. Staying that long in wolf form always made my muscles sore.

“Hold on.” He tossed the crab into the fire

and stood. "Why is my sister in Farrow's Gate and not at home? She would never leave our firehawks."

"We don't have time." I turned to leave, and he grabbed my arm. I stilled, glaring at the human.

"You need to start talking." His grip on me tightened and if he wasn't Rosalie's brother, I would've forcefully removed him.

"Fine, but then we need to go. I've already been gone too long." As quickly as possible, I re-told the story of how she arrived at Farrow's Gate, the problem with the snakes, the flock, the marriage, and how Kelia had come to take all the prospects away.

When I had finished, he rubbed his chin, deep in thought. "I need to go home."

"Didn't you hear me? Rosalie is in danger."

"Yes, but you said Kelia left and Lord Demious was protecting Rosy. We'll check there first before going to the Borderlands. Even if Kelia managed to get my sister, no one is going into battle. The darkthings decimated the base camp. Thousands of soldiers wiped out. The magi won't risk anymore until the final push. We have time, but the firehawks don't. They're integral to the North and not just because of the plague snakes."

He clapped a hand on my shoulder. "We need

to pass that way anyway to reach Farrow's Gate and if Lord Demious is as powerful as you say, he can port us to the Borderlands faster than we can travel."

"Very well," I grumbled, not happy with this plan. Though, knowing how important the fowl were to Rosalie, I needed to make sure they were safe.

"There's a good lad." He playfully smacked my cheek, and I grabbed his throat.

"Do not touch me again, *human*." Gripping his throat, I applied pressure.

"Understood, personal space. Got it."

Releasing him, I sighed, already annoyed.

"You know," he said as he held his hands over the fire pulling the flames into his palms until the entire fire vanished. "It would be a lot faster if you gave me a lift."

I growled and he pretended not to laugh.

"I'm just stating the facts. You do want to get to my sister faster, don't you?"

Even if he was right, the idea of a human riding me sent a wave of anger through me. My swiftness ability was faster than when I was in wolf form but couldn't be maintained over long distances. No matter how much I loathed it, the human was right.

"We stop when I need to and that's it."

The human held out his hand. "Calvin."

Shaking his hand, I replied. "Baine."

"Okay, Baine. Let's get moving. If we hurry, we can make it to my home in two days."

Two days.

That wasn't fast enough.

Noticing my apprehension, the human's expression shifted to understanding. "She's my twin. No one is more important than her. I wouldn't risk going home if I didn't believe with my every fiber the magi wouldn't put her into battle. You need to trust me."

"Then let's go."

Shifting into wolf form, I ignored the uneasiness of letting a human ride me and kept Rosalie in my thoughts. The faster I ran, the closer I came to getting her back into my arms, and I'd already been gone too long.

With the human on my back, I ran, through forest and hills and plains covered with grass too high to see where I traveled. We stopped twice to rest before quickly returning to the road.

My companion said little, seemingly lost in deep thought. His previous temperament disappeared into the long silence of our journey. When we had crossed into the North by the mountains, he patted my side.

"Follow that river, east. We're close."

The river snaked around the hills and through the deep wood. Patches of beige peppered the green grass. I slid to a stop when the ground morphed into a brackish mud littered with dead snakes.

Calvin jumped off and I transformed, feeling uneasy being in my wolf form this long.

He kneeled and poked one of the dead snakes. "They're dead. Are all of them dead?"

"Are these the plague snakes Rosalie spoke about?"

He nodded, his brow knit together, and he frowned. "Yes, but what would have killed them all?"

Walking ahead, he stepped slowly, eyeing the area. The river we followed decreased in size as we made our way deeper into the forest. Stepping behind Calvin, I surveyed the area carefully, wondering what caused the odd patches of brown and black among the foliage.

This wasn't like the barren waste caused by the darkthings. There was a sickness in this forest, a stench underneath the fresh air.

Calvin ran, making me give chase. Ahead, a wooden bridge crossed over the river leading to a dirt road that wound around large oaks. He ran across the bridge, quickening his pace as he disappeared on the road. Using my swiftness, I caught up to him instantly. His brows raised in surprise, but he continued, a desperate look in his gaze as the road led to a thatched house surrounded by a wooden fence and nestled between a barn and another larger fenced in structure.

Vaulting over the fence, he headed to the structure that resembled a chicken coop but on a larger scale. He froze, a strangled "no" slipped from his mouth as he dropped to his knees.

"What is it?" I said, peeking into the empty structure.

"They're all gone . . ."

"Your sister mentioned a ranger. He may be here." Using my senses, I searched for signs of life.

An acrid scent caught my attention and I headed to the house. I had no swords, no weapon except my hands. They would need to be enough. Putting my ear to the door, I listened.

Snores. Someone was sleeping inside.

Whistling low, I called Calvin to my side. Fire brimmed in his eyes, matching the intensity of his hardened expression. Slowly, I turned the doorknob and stepped in.

An old man slept on the couch, bundled in blankets.

"Necker?" Calvin walked in, the fire vanishing from his gaze.

"Huh? Who's there?" The old man rubbed his face and white beard, suddenly awake and a bit lost.

"It's Calvin."

"Calvin? Is it really you?" The old man stood, straightening his white shirt and fixing his pants.

"It is." The two hugged, Calvin at least a head taller than the old man. "What happened? Where are all the firehawks?"

"Come." Calvin followed the man into a bedroom. "I moved the last one into your parents' bedroom, wanted to keep her and her eggs safe."

He opened the door and on the bed sat a large hawk, red and orange feathers created a shimmering effect, and a tuft of purple plumes adorned the top of the bird's head. The hawk lifted its head and Calvin smiled.

"Henrietta." Calvin sat next to the fowl and stroked the bird's side. It cooed at him. "You were always the strongest one."

"Is Miss Rose with ya? She told me to watch the hawks but then never came back. People at the market said one of the traders took her."

"No." Calvin's shoulder sagged, and he leaned over to kiss the hawk on top of her head. "But I'm going to get her, but after you tell me what happened to our flock. Is Henrietta really the only one left?"

"I'm sorry, Master Hawk." The older human shook his head. "The snakes kept coming and every night more of the firehawks were killed or died off. Everything here is tainted. I brought this one when I noticed she laid eggs and kept her safe."

"The snakes we passed are all dead," I said, moving to step around the bed and look out the round window. "What killed them?"

"All of them? That can't be. How?" The human joined me and peered outside, squinting. "Our prayers have been answered. The All Father has blessed us!"

Suddenly, with a loud, excited yelp, the old man rushed out of the bedroom then outside to where we were just looking. He pointed at the grass, bending down, and clapping his hands before stomping on something I couldn't see.

"This is who your sister left in charge?"

Calvin sighed. "Necker is a family friend. He's a bit eccentric but he's trustworthy."

Though I was curious to see more of where Rosalie grew up, I knew time was not on our side. "Calvin."

"I know. Give me a few moments to gather supplies and prepare Henrietta."

"Prepare?" I stared at the bird who lifted its beak toward Calvin's hand.

"Yes, she and the eggs are coming with us. She's the last of the firehawks from the North. She's more important than you or I."

"How do you suggest we travel without upsetting the eggs?"

Calvin's lip curved upward, and he gave me a glance from head to toe. "You think you could pull a cart while you run?"

Rage vibrated through my body and if the mother hawk wasn't resting beside him, I'd punch the human hard enough to teach him a bit of respect. "Be careful with your words, human."

Laughing, Calvin stood and met my furious gaze. "You're the one who fell for my sister. I'm deciding if you're worthy enough to keep her."

TWENTY-SIX

ROSALIE

My head ached and even the slightest movement hurt. I groaned and dragged the blanket over my head to block out the light. “Do you have to open them?”

“You’ve been sleeping most of the day,” Ara said. “I’d think you’d be famished by now.”

“I certainly am.” Janetta tugged at the blanket. “Come on, Rosalie. I want to eat, and I don’t want to go downstairs alone. Ms. Begalia is going to make us do something ridiculous. I just know it.”

“Ugh. Fine.” Tossing the blanket off, I stretched, every muscle hurting. “I feel awful.”

Janetta sat on the edge of the bed. She’d

come into my room late last night and hadn't left. Everyone was upset and nervous. We had no idea what was going to happen. Even if Marco said he would protect us, we still didn't belong here.

"Here. I know how much you hate the ones with tight bodices." Ara placed a long navy dress on the bed. The edges had the slightest ruffle and the neckline reached down a bit farther than I liked, but it wasn't constrained by strings or something more horrid.

"I'm going to get dressed. I'll meet you by the kitchen, and don't take too long. I am ravenous." Janetta hopped off the bed and waved goodbye to Ara as she left.

"I will."

As Ara helped me dress and brush out my hair, I thought of Baine. That portal led to the Borderlands, a place of death and darkness and no matter how hard I tried to reconcile in my head that Baine was fae and he'd be fine, my heart ached with worry. In saving me, he'd doomed himself.

"I'm sure he's okay," Ara whispered as she braided my hair. Without me saying anything, she knew.

Picking at my nails, I nodded. "I hope so. What will happen now with Lord Demious gone?"

"I don't know. It's not your concern. Marco will keep his word. There. You look beautiful." Grabbing my shoulders, she turned me toward the floor-length mirror, smiling behind me. "Everything will work out. You'll see, miss."

Taking her hand, I squeezed it. "Thank you."

Her cheeks reddened, and I wondered if anyone had thanked her before.

My stomach grumbled loud, and we both laughed.

"Come on," she said, smiling wide. "Before that belly of yours wakes the whole house."

Janetta waved from the bottom of the long steps, and I ran to her. Her long brown hair hung loose around her shoulders and the olive dress she wore flowed around her like liquid silk. "Took you long enough."

Looping my arm around hers, I spun us toward the kitchens. "You could have gone ahead."

Leaning into me, she sighed. "I know. I don't want to be alone though."

"I'm going to rush ahead and see if the cook made any of those honey buns with the cinnamon glaze," Ara whispered behind us.

These two women had become friends and leaving them was something I wasn't ready to do. I'd been alone for so long, I'd forgotten what it was like to need someone.

The doors to the main entrance burst open, wood splintering into sharp shards. The three of us screamed. Two figures in black cloaks, covering everything but their red eyes floated toward us.

"Go!" I pushed Janetta ahead of me, toward the kitchen.

One of the figures suddenly appeared behind me, grabbing me around the waist with one hand and locking a metal object around my neck with the other.

"No!" I kicked and clawed at my attacker, feeling my flame being snuffed out.

With frightening speed, we flew out the broken entrance to where a massive beaked monster stood outside, black tattered rags hung off its body. My heartbeat quickened with fear.

In horror, I was dragged to the creature from the tower. Janetta screamed, reflecting my own fears. My heart beat loudly in my ears, the terror of being eaten by the crone sending my head into a spiral.

"Bring herrrr to meeee." The crone lifted a taloned finger and curled it, beckoning its minion to bring me closer.

A portal to my left opened. Borderlands Agents flowed out, followed by a familiar blonde-haired woman. The crone hissed at the incoming crowd.

"What are you doing crone?" Kelia asked and flicked a hand, ordering her men to surround us.

A female fae, dressed in leather with weapons hanging on every side, walked with Kelia. The bottom of the fae's face was shrouded in a black mask and her brown hair was pulled back in various braids. She unsheathed two daggers.

"Magiii . . . you will not interfereeee." The crone pointed at Kelia. "Keep your assassin awayyyyy."

The brown skinned fae glanced at Kelia before stepping around and heading toward me.

"You have no authority here. The magi have claimed that human and I will take her." Kelia's hands glowed blue.

"The Magistrate is deaaddd."

"What? How?" Kelia held up a hand, making the fae who was only a foot away from me pause.

"We didn't seeee," the crone said, hobbling forward, its back humped. "I felt the magic leave."

"This is problematic." Kelia's hands stopped glowing. "What do you want with that human?"

Marco and the remaining guards came from the side of the estate, flanking the soldiers. Even with all of them here, the Borderlands Agents were too many. My gaze went to Janetta who had tears in her eyes. She stood inside the broken entryway; her emotions painted all over her frightened face.

"We will sacrifice the elementallll," the crone said, revealing my heritage and causing the people around me to whisper. "The next moon cycle is almost uponnn ussss. Her sacrifice will feeeddd the barrierrr until another magistrate is founnddd."

Kelia nodded. "Take her to the tower. I will meet you there."

"No!" Janetta ran forward, but Marco grabbed her. "You can't do this!"

Marco whispered in her ear, holding her tight to his chest.

She struggled, tears flowing freely.

"It's okay," I said, holding back the urge to cry. "Marco will get you home like he promised, right?"

The dark fae nodded, his jaw clenched. He kept his arms tight around Janetta, holding her back.

The portal re-opened, and the Borderlands Agents disappeared first.

"Are you sure about this?" the female fae said to Kelia.

"We don't have any other option right now."

"The magi won't be pleased."

"Go, Raina, and stop reminding me of the facts."

The females disappeared, the portal closing behind them.

A loud caw brought my attention to the crone who unfurled large wings and tore off into the sky. The cloaked figures holding me, floated upward, taking me away from the estate.

Janetta screamed, cried, the sound piercing my soul.

I didn't dare look back, because if I did, the tears would never stop.

TWENTY-SEVEN

BAINE

Turning on to the road that led to the estate, my heart did an odd thump. It had been almost a week since I had left Farrow's Gate. My traveling companion sat next to me on the bench, quietly, the bird soaring above us, the satchel of eggs on his lap. He'd been silent since we crossed through the barrier. Neither of us knew what to expect, and I assumed his decision to not come here quicker, pained him by the tightened brow and how he hadn't made a joke since last night.

I'd been preparing myself for the worst.

As long as Rosalie lived, everything else could be fixed. I would not allow Lord Demious to wed her. He would not give her up easily and

I was prepared to fight. Nothing would stop me from returning to her arms.

"How much longer," Calvin asked, his tone matching his dark countenance.

"Once we crest this hill—"

I halted my horse, stopping us as my men raced up the hill on horseback, Marco in the lead. He pulled up alongside us.

"What's happened?" I stood, ready to leap off the wagon."

He took a sheath from around his neck and tossed me my twin swords. "The crone took her. You need to go now."

"The crone? Why?"

"Demious is dead."

Though I heard him say it, my mind couldn't comprehend it. Demious dead? Impossible?

"Baine! Go to the tower, now. The crone is going to sacrifice her."

"Is he talking about my sister?" Calvin's gaze flared red. "Where is my sister?"

The horses neighed as Calvin's fury manifested in licking flames off his hands.

"Stay here," I ordered Marco. "We can handle the crone."

Marco nodded and turned the horse around, whistling to the other men to follow.

With a slap of the reins, I urged the horse to race toward the tower.

"You need to start talking to me. What's this crone and why does it want my sister?"

"There is a magical barrier surrounding Farrow's Gate. It contains the wild magic. If the barrier falls, it will call every darkthing here and no one knows what the wild magic will do."

"So why don't we do whatever spell or ritual we need and keep it up?"

The firehawk cawed in the sky above us.

"It takes an immense amount of magical energy to energize the barrier. Lord Demious was unique in that his shadow magic was unparalleled. We need time to find a replacement. We have to kill the crone. It won't let Rosalie go."

"Great, save my sister and destroy the world. Fabulous life choices." Calvin frowned and I shared his sentiment. "What's the plan?"

"First we need to drop off the eggs. The crone will want to eat them if they're in the Tower."

Calvin's eyes widened in horror, and he hugged the satchel closer to his chest.

"I have a friend who will help us."

Enola would not approve of killing the crone. The creature spent its entire life in the tower, testing the magic in the surrounding lands, watching for anomalies and danger that couldn't be seen with the naked eye. It was impervious to magic, and hard to kill due to its size and thick coat. It was one thing to subdue a crone, another to end its pitiful existence.

Avoiding the fear and worry banging against my thoughts, I focused on heading to Moonlake and Enola's cottage. We had one day before the next moon cycle. Enough time to rescue Rosalie, but not to save Farrow's Gate.

Enola's goat bleated as I pulled the wagon to a stop outside the flowered home. Calvin cawed at his bird, calling the hawk to his outstretched arm. Enola opened the door, her expression solemn and gaze tired. Without a word, she reached out to me, and I embraced my old friend.

"He's gone," I said, holding her.

"I know."

"The crone has Rosalie."

"I know." Enola pulled away from me. "You can't save her."

"Enola . . ." I growled, but the human did not cower, instead she placed a hand on my cheek.

"Farrow's Gate will fall." Her words pierced my heart.

"You can't ask this of me," I spat back. "I will not sacrifice her. I *can't* allow it."

Understanding dawned in Enola's gaze. "You foolish fae. Out of all the souls in this world, you've chosen hers."

Taking Enola's hand off my face, I gripped it, unafraid of the truth I now knew in my heart.

"There has to be another way."

"If I may," Calvin said, inserting himself into the conversation. "I may have a solution that will save my sister and this place."

"Sister?" Enola released me and eyed my companion. "No, not just sister, twin."

"You noticed my dashing looks, have you? My sister gets it from me." Calvin smiled wide, and though I had not known the human long, I had learned that his devious smile usually meant he had an idea I would not agree with it.

"Baine stop glaring. Both of you come inside where we can speak freely." Enola pushed me forward.

The firehawk stayed on Calvin's arm and Enola stopped to admire the bird. Inside her home, she cooed at the hawk, motioning it to an area near the fire. Calvin slipped off the satchel and placed it on the floor near a pile of thick crocheted blankets. "These are her eggs. They're very fragile."

Enola nodded, kneeling next to Calvin, creating a nest out of the blankets. "She'll be safe here. I have some worms I keep for bait in the shed."

"Thank you," Calvin said, cooing to the firehawk that nestled on top of her eggs.

"If you two are finished, we need to discuss Rosalie."

"Is he always so grumpy?" Calvin whispered to Enola.

"He's getting worse in his old age."

"Enough!" My emotions were raw, and I could not wait a moment longer.

"You were the one who said we had a day, and I have a plan." Calvin stood, making his way over to the table where a decanter sat. "Is that wine?"

"Yes, help yourself," Enola said, grabbing mugs from a shelf on the wall.

As Calvin poured himself a drink, I was moments away from wrapping my hands around his throat. Rage pumped through my veins. I could not sit here idly chatting a moment more.

Unphased by my pacing or snarling, Calvin drank before speaking. "You said the barrier around Farrow's Gate needs a lot of power. Me and my sister can help it. Teach us how and we'll maintain it."

"Impossible," I said. "Though you're both strong, you need unbridled magic."

"I've got the elemental kind." He winked and Enola gasped.

"Elemental? Twin elementals?" Enola's eyes shined. "That's why the crone wanted to eat her?"

"Eat her?" Calvin's gaze bounced between me and Enola.

Enola turned to me, her face lighting up with hope. I didn't want to believe it. Could we be that lucky? "Will it work?"

Her smiled widened. "It could. If we knew the ritual to perform, yes."

"But we don't. Who does?"

"I bet you the magi do," Calvin said in between bites. He found a loaf of bread and bit into it. "Either of you know how to contact them?"

Enola placed a hand on my arm. "We don't need to. They'll be here to watch the crone and make sure the creature sacrifices Rosalie."

"Then we wait," I said, the hope I dared to believe in taking fruit inside my heart. "We make our move during the ritual tomorrow."

"Great, now who else needs a drink?" Calvin held up the decanter and I grabbed a mug off the table.

"Pour."

TWENTY-EIGHT

ROSALIE

The musty scent of the cell gave me the worst headache, adding to the dismal décor. With my flame snuffed out and no one who cared to come save me, I tried my best to deal with the reality of the situation.

I was going to die.

The crone didn't give me details and I didn't want to know any.

Would it hurt?

If I was lucky, and I didn't think luck existed in my life, the pain would be minimal.

Curling into a ball on the hard cot, I hugged my knees to my chest, thinking of Baine, my brother, my home. When Calvin returned from war, and I refused to believe he wouldn't, he'd come back to everything gone. The firehawks would never survive and he would have no idea that I sold myself into death.

So many mistakes.

Why did I leave the farm? I should've stayed home.

Tears fell and I let them streak my dirty face.

There was nothing more left inside me.

They'd broken whatever hope or will I still had.

Now I was nothing but a human sacrifice.

Maybe in death I could be useful.

Jingling keys brought my attention to the empty corridor. The cells were in the dungeon, deep below the tower where stone and decay laid rest. The glow of an oil lamp crept closer, followed by the shuffling of feet. One of the crone's cloaked minions came to my cell, a glowing rod in one of its hands. I hate that I couldn't see their face. Just those creepy red eyes surrounded by a black shroud.

With one hand, it opened the cell door and with the other pointed the rod at me.

A blue energy zapped my body and I screamed, clutching myself in pain. I bit my lip as my muscles convulsed. The figure moved inside the cell, faster than I expected and unhooked the chain around the floor.

The chain connected to the cuffs around my

ankles and my wrists. With a yank, it pulled the chain forward, making me tumble off the cot and slam into the stone. I cried out as my chin bled from the impact. Taking the chain in my hands, I tried to pull, but my muscles trembled and any strength I had disappeared from the blast of that rod.

"Walk." The voice sounded oddly human.

Realizing fighting was pointless, I stood, my legs shaking, and shuffled behind the odd creature or person. I couldn't tell.

Slowly, we walked up the dimly lit stairs, round and round, all the way up. Twice, I had to lean against the side of the wall to catch my breath. I had never felt so weak. Everything hurt, my throat ached with dryness and dizziness made every step more treacherous than the next.

How long had we been climbing these stairs? They seemed to go on forever. Glancing down, my stomach dropped. I couldn't see the bottom anymore, just a black hole. Moving closer to the wall, I followed the cloaked figure in front of me, desperate to get off these stairs.

We ended at a door with a lock on it. The thing in front of me used a key from the ring and unlocked the door. Sunlight filled the stairwell and I squinted against the sharp light. With another tug, I stumbled through the doorway and onto the top of the tower.

Jagged spires surrounded the circular structure. In the center of the ground laid two crystal pillars that sparkled and created rainbows. A beautiful image that didn't belong in this moment.

There was no one else up here which I found odd. Where was the crone?

When did they plan to kill me?

On the ground between the two pillars was a stone circle, strange shapes and script carved into it. The hooded creature took my chain and looped it through a hook in the middle of the intricate designs.

"What are you doing?" I pulled on the chain, but the thick metal barely budged.

Without a word, the hooded figure turned and walked back through the door, leaving me alone, chained between two pillars.

Sitting on the ground, I looked around, wondering what would happen next.

A black shadow from the sky moved at frightening speed toward the tower. At the same time, a portal opened up and Kelia stepped out, right next to the pillar on the left of me. The black shape landed on the tower, enormous black wings curling back.

The crone.

"Did you bring ittttt?" It clacked at Kelia, scuttling across the stone like a vulture.

"The magi are not pleased with this decision," she said, eyeing me before taking a vial out of the pocket in her white dress. She seemed too sweet and gentle, adorned in a white gown that accentuated her perfectly. How could someone like her be involved with a monster like the crone?

The two of them walked forward and I slid away, locked in place by the chains. Kelia kneeled on the ground and grabbed my face. "Drink."

Clamping my mouth shut, I shook my head.

The crone hissed and came behind me, grabbing my braid between its talons and yanking my head back so much I screamed. Kelia poured the liquid into my mouth and covered my mouth and nose, forcing me to swallow.

"The tincture should work in a few minutes." Kelia wiped her hand off on a handkerchief she pulled from her cloak. "Then you can remove her collar without any interference."

The crone clacked and hissed, making an odd noise as it moved to one of the pillars and began tapping various parts of it.

The liquid warmed my belly and the tension in my muscles disappeared within the sunlight that seemed to radiate inside me. With a yawn, I laid my cheek against the stone, the chill of it feeling like a cool drink.

Kelia placed a hand on my forehead, her

touch sent a tingling sensation through my face and down to my toes. "It's working. Her body temperature is rising."

"What did you do to me?" I licked my lips, my mouth dry and too hot.

"It's a potent tonic that will remove any fear and make your body feel out of sorts." She kept her gaze locked to mine. Her icy blue eyes seemed out of place, too piercing and cold to come from a woman with such a warm touch.

"Why . . . why are you doing this?" I licked my lips again and blinked the dizziness from my eyes. Every time I tried to focus on her, my eyes twitched, and I had to close them to regain some sense of stability.

"It's our only option." Her voice sounded distant, getting further away. "Farrow's Gate cannot fall."

I suddenly didn't care about the whispers around me or the chains or even death. The sadness drifted away into the puffy clouds in the sky. When Kelia came back over to me, I could barely move, not that I wanted to anyway. She leaned over and unclasped my collar, talking to the crone, her words fuzzy in my ear.

She asked me a question, but I couldn't follow what she said.

"Huh?" Lifting my face off the stone, I rubbed my hand over my neck, the sensation of my fingers against skin sending me into bliss.

Kelia grabbed me from under my shoulders and hoisted me to my feet. I slumped against her body which was warm and soft. Leaning my head on her shoulder, I rested, staring at the beautiful sky.

"Can you chain her to the pillars?" Kelia said, moving to hold me around my waist.

"You magi don't knowwww how to creaattteee the right potionssss." The crone yanked me away from Kelia and I frowned.

In the sky two shapes soared in and out of the clouds streaks of red and yellow making beautiful painted strokes in the air. The image reminded me of that time in the gardens where the ash raptors whisked me off into the air. As if my mind conjured him into being, a vision of Baine riding an ash raptor flew in the sky, coming closer.

The potion they gave me must be causing hallucinations.

Talons raked my skin, but it didn't hurt.

Kelia tugged my cuffed hands in front of me, arguing with the crone about the right way to position me.

None of it mattered because my last thoughts were playing out in front of me.

I get to see you one last time.

A single tear slid down my cheek and I smiled.

Not because I was about to be slaughtered, but because I wasn't going into the Never alone. Baine had come to say goodbye.

I don't care that you're not real.

I'm going to tell you what I should've said before.

The image hovered over the tower now. Baine unsheathed two swords, face taught with anger and then he leapt from the back of the bird to fall behind Kelia. Another ash raptor shrieked in the sky, this one bringing someone I did not expect, even if I was hallucinating.

Calvin?

My brother jumped off the back of the raptor, turning into flames before he landed.

The crone hissed and launched forward. Kelia swung around, blue magic pouring from out of her hands. Baine disappeared, too quick for me to follow. Kelia and the crone turned their attention to the firestorm heading toward them.

Baine appeared in front of me, those hypnotic lavender eyes dragging me out of the nightmare.

"You can't be real," I said, my mind struggling to believe what my eyes could see.

"I am." He pressed his mouth to mine, fast and fierce, awakening my flame which burned through the fog in my mind.

"You came for me?"

Grabbing the chain between the handcuffs, he

yanked it apart, setting me free. "I will *always* come for you."

Before I could comprehend the situation, something looped around Baine's neck and yanked him on to his back. Kelia dragged Baine across the stone.

"No!" I ran forward, begging my flame to spark but whatever tonic they had given me kept my magic shackled. "Please, stop!"

Baine flipped over, the noose tightening around his neck. He sliced one of his swords across Kelia's calves, but the metal hit an invisible barrier. "There's another way!"

"What are you talking about?" Kelia twisted her arm, flipping Baine forward and raising him to his knees.

Slipping his fingers under the magical noose, he eyed Kelia. "Rosalie and her twin can power the barrier."

Kelia glanced over at my brother who was unrecognizable under the flames. The crone launched at him, Calvin's flames not burning a single feather. "Being able to wield fire does not make one powerful."

"No," he coughed and stood, glaring at Kelia. "But being half elemental does."

"Impossible."

"It's true!" I ran in front of Baine, holding out my arms. "No one else knows but our parents.

My father was an elemental. He swore us to secrecy."

Baine coughed and gasped behind me.

"Please," I begged, falling to my knees. "Don't kill him. I'll do whatever you want. I'll stay in Farrow's Gate. We'll help. You said the magi didn't like this plan anyway."

"Baine! I could use some help over here!" my brother yelled, the flames making him indistinguishable. The crone grabbed his shirt and threw him into one of the spires, cracking the stone. My brother's flames spouted out and he went silent.

I couldn't lose the two most important people in my life.

"Kelia. Give us a chance, please," I begged.

She stepped back and released her magic. "You will have your chance."

With a relieved smile I turned around.

Baine's eyes widened in shock and his hand went to his stomach.

The crone cackled. "You will all die herreeeee."

Blood coated the crone's talons and it screeched as Baine fell forward into me.

"No, no, this can't be happening." My body shook as Baine coughed blood onto my dress.

"Go. Kelia will keep her word. I'll keep the crone busy."

"No! I'm not leaving you." With my arms

around him, I held him up, refusing to leave his side.

"I love you," Baine whispered in my ear. "Now, run."

Pushing away from me, Baine picked up his sword and ran forward, blood splattering the stone with his steps. The crone rushed forward, talons out.

Fire erupted inside me, drowning out the fear and worry.

Rage awakened my flame into a frenzy until my body consisted of nothing but fire. Running, I sprinted past Baine and to the crone, shooting out a fireball and screaming.

The ball of fire sent the crone flying backward, but I didn't stop. Keeping the momentum, I jumped at the monster, flames digging into its feathered body. It snapped its beak at me and using all my strength, I pushed my magic into its chest, forcing through the barrier that kept the fire out.

The spire broke behind the creature and it tumbled over the edge, me on top.

Baine screamed my name.

Unleashing my magic fully, I let the fire blaze around me, disintegrating my clothes and dressing me in flames until the crone's beaked face began to melt as it shrieked in agony. Something snatched me away from the crone right before the monster cracked against the ground, black ichor oozing from its head.

An ash raptor flew around the tower, away from the broken body of the crone and over to where the grass swayed. When the bird placed me on the grass, I called back the flames and gazed up at the tower.

Baine . . .

Wind wrapped around me, until the breeze materialized into the fae who had stolen more than my heart. He wrapped his arms around my naked body, hugging me to his chest. “You’re alive.”

“For now,” I said and pulled back to examine his wound. “But you’re hurt.”

He tugged his shirt over his head and pulled it over mine. “I’ll heal.”

My eyes watered and he grabbed my face with his hands. “Is it over?”

“Yes, and I swear to you now, I will never leave you again.” With that promise, he kissed me, and I let the fear of what would happen next fade away.

TWENTY-NINE

ROSALIE

Calvin, Baine, and I stood in the center of the maze garden where the rocks spiraled around a dirt patch on the ground. There wasn't anything special about this area, at least none that I could see. Calvin and I wore matching blue robes. The thick material made me itch and sweat, but Baine told us Lord Demious wore only this when he performed his meditation out here.

Having my brother back home filled me with relief. He glanced over and winked at me.

The moment we were reunited, I wanted to spend hours talking with him, but there was no time for reconnecting until the barrier around Farrow's Gate was secured.

"What are we supposed to actually do here?" Calvin scratched the back of his head as he stared at the ground.

Baine had been extremely brief on how Calvin and I could maintain the wards surrounding Farrow's Gate. Even after all my incessant prodding on our way here, he was extremely tight lipped about the whole ordeal. I wasn't sure if he knew or if he did and he regretted allowing Calvin and I to stay and help. Not like we had a choice. I doubted Kelia would've agreed to step aside during the fight with the crone otherwise.

Behind Calvin a bright whirl of light began circling into the air, the color swirling blue until the air disappeared and an oval opening showed a woman with stark blonde hair wearing a black dress with red trim along the edges and a red patch on her chest.

Kelia stepped through the portal alone, her gaze fixated on Calvin. He smiled wide at her like the two were long lost friends.

"You should have revealed your heritage early on," she said, seeming unphased by my brother's charm. "The magi have agreed to allow you and your sister to maintain the barrier."

Breathing a sigh of relief, I looked at my brother. We could do this.

Kelia's blank expression was as icy as her blue eyes. "Sit in the center, there, and hold hands."

Calvin arched a brow at me, but begrudgingly sat on the dirt circle. Baine stepped aside, keeping both hands on the hilts of the swords hanging on his hips, his brow furrowed with concern.

"Do we sing now?" Calvin joked, his wide smile almost making me laugh.

I squeezed his hands and didn't miss the stern gaze Kelia sent our way.

"Ouch," he whispered.

"Stop acting like a child." I wondered how my twin could even joke at a time like this.

"You must perform the ritual at the exact time the sun hits the horizon," Kelia said. "Or you fail to keep this land safe."

I eyed my brother, begging him to focus.

He nodded and closed his eyes. "We're ready."

"Search for the power inside you then release it into the ground as deep as you can reach."

With my eyes closed, I focused on my flame, the spark that made me feel alive, the fire that had kept me warm when nothing surrounded me but darkness.

"Release it," Kelia said.

Warmth spread through my core, my arms, my hands, almost as if the connection with my twin would swirl us up into a tornado of fire. An unnatural wind picked up my hair and swirled it around my face. Calvin's grip on me tightened, our hands burning as one flame.

"Into the ground," Kelia shouted beside us. "Focus the energy below you, nowhere else."

Her loud voice pushed me to action. Gathering the vortex inside my body into a single mass, I shoved my power low, to my legs, lower, the energy funneling through me like a conduit.

A bolt of electric ripped through my body, melding my hands to Calvin. I screamed, opening my eyes, but could see nothing but flames, my vision hazed and unfocused. Calvin yelled with me, but didn't let go, his vicelike grip keeping us connected.

"What's happening?" Baine yelled. "What are you doing to them?"

"Nothing. This is how the barrier is maintained."

I screamed as pain ripped through my body, shredding my insides.

"Is this what the magi planned?" Baine growled. "Are you going to sacrifice them?"

My thoughts hazed as my head grew lighter, dazed. The energy coursing through me and my twin was too much.

Was I going to die?

Was Calvin?

"Calvin," I croaked.

"I'm here," he grunted, holding my hands.

"Enough, Baine! You will not interfere. This must be done."

I couldn't see what was happening around us. Everything began to get hazy, meshing my thoughts, my mind. It all grew weary.

Water. I need water.

A drink

Something . . . to . . . stop . . . the pain.

Something growled, then whimpered.

And then silence.

I was going to kill her.

Tear her to pieces.

Kelia held a magical lasso around my neck, and even in wolf form, I couldn't move. The only thing I cared about in this forsaken world was dying in front of me and I was helpless to stop it.

I'd been tricked. How could I think the magi would agree to any bargain? What I couldn't understand was what was the purpose of this ritual? Farrow's Gate wasn't just another land, it bred wild magic, and no one knew what that wild magic would do if left uncontrolled. We were fools to think the magi would honor anything.

Rage consumed my body, heating me to the point that the burning noose around my neck did little to slow me down. I put one paw forward, inching closer toward the human I'd fallen for.

"No." Kelia yanked on the noose, treating me like a domesticated beast.

Fine. I'll bite you instead.

Without hesitation, I turned and leaped at Kelia, taking her off guard. She stumbled back but was quick enough to throw her free hand up and create a barrier that I slammed into.

The knock didn't faze me, and I shook the hit off, stalking forward, growling, and letting her know she wouldn't survive this encounter. There was no fear in her eyes, no regret, nothing but the cold hard determination of a stubborn human with a mission.

"Keep your paws off me or I will portal you into a mud pit in the vile south."

Her threat did nothing. What did I care of being sent somewhere where decay and acrid rotting vegetation covered everything, when my heart was being destroyed in front of me?

"She will live. They both will." Kelia swirled her hand in a circle, creating a swirling mass of blue light. "Now, sit."

With a flick of her wrist, she hurled the glowing sphere at my face, knocking me backward and off my feet. The side of my face stung, and my muscles spasmed. I lay on the stone, my body convulsing.

The circle where Rosalie and Calvin sat was a cone of flame. I couldn't see anything but their silhouettes. Rosalie had stopped screaming and lay slumped over her brother.

My heart ached.

No, not ached, *broke.*

Burned hair filled the air and my eyes watered at the smoke lifting from the center of that cone. The cyclone of fire shot up into the sky, blasting through the clouds. A beam of blue light coursed from the circle on the ground, pulsing, shimmering magic up into the sky. The colors swirled high above the clouds and spread out as far as I could see, until all at once, everything stopped.

With the fire gone, I could finally see Rosalie and Calvin. They still held hands, but slumped over each other, eyes closed, clothes smoking. At least the robes Lord Demious used for this ritual seemed magical.

Kelia released the noose around my neck. "They will need rest."

Shaking out the dazed feeling in my body, I rolled to a sitting position until the numbing sensation dissipated, and I could shift back into my fae form. "What happened?"

I moved to Rosalie's side, but she burned, and this time she was too hot to touch.

"It will get easier for them. They must perform this at the same time, every third cycle of the moon. They'll be fine in a few minutes." Kelia took out a rod and waved it in the air.

"You're leaving?"

"There's nothing more for me to do here. The magi are not your enemy. It would do you well to remember that." The portal opened and she stepped through, disappearing, and leaving me with many questions.

"Baine!" Marco ran toward me, out of breath. "What was that? I was out by the eastern gate when I saw something shoot into the sky. Whoa, are they?"

"They're alive." I reached out to touch Rosalie's face. The heat had lessened, making her skin warm but not scolding. "I don't understand what happened. Lord Demious did nothing like this."

Marco kneeled beside me. "Different powers. I don't know. Should we move them?"

Slipping Rosalie into my arms, I stood. "Take him inside to his room and have the servants tend to him."

"Where are you going?"

"To the lake."

THIRTY-ONE

ROSALIE

Cool water caressed my limbs. I opened my eyes to see the clear sky.

"You're finally awake." Baine smiled above me.

"Where? What?" Looking around, we were at the Moonlake or rather in the lake. Baine held me in his arms in the water, which reached up to his chest. Everything from my chest down submerged in the refreshing water.

"After the ritual I took you here to cool down."

"Calvin?"

"He's safe. Marco took him inside and the servants are tending to him."

My head pounded, a dull ache that pinched the bridge of my nose and my forehead. "I feel horrible."

"I thought you were dying in front of me."

Shifting my body slightly, I stared into Baine's light eyes and lifted a hand to brush his cheek. He turned in to my touch, closing his eyes.

"Kelia's powerful, more powerful than any magi I know of. I couldn't do anything to stop what was happening. I thought the magic you and your brother cast would kill you both."

"Did it work?"

He shook his head, looking lost and broken. "I don't know. There's no way to know until it's too late and the darkthings arrive. You can't do that again though. How can you?"

Wrapping an arm around his shoulders, I placed my feet onto the sand, my toes squishing into the bottom of the lake. "What if I have to?"

"No, I don't care."

With both my arms around his neck, I forced him to look at me. "We can't ignore our duties, no matter how difficult."

Baine slid his hands to my waist, gripping my hips. "You don't understand what it felt like. What it feels like for a fae to lose his mate."

"Your what?"

My heart fluttered. Baine and I hadn't had time to talk about us, not with everything that had happened. I knew he cared about me, even wanted me, but mate? I didn't even think it was possible for a fae to be mated to a human.

His eyes widened, the realization of what he just admitted dawning on his blushing face. "Uh . . . well . . . I . . ."

Biting my lip, I smiled. "You called me your mate. Do you really mean that?"

"We should go eat. I'm sure you're hungry." Moving away from me, he walked out of the lake and over to an area by the shore where a blanket and a basket had been set out.

"Baine!" Grabbing my wet robe, I trampled out of the water and over to the grass.

"Enola made cheese rolls and brought you a clean outfit to change into. I'll give you some privacy." He turned his back to me, water sliding down his bare back, accentuating the corded muscles. He'd gone into the lake wearing only a pair of black pants.

He could ignore the question for a few minutes, but only because I really was hungry and soaked. Slipping out of the robes, I quickly threw on the blue cotton dress. "Finished."

Not wanting to look at how amazing he looked without a shirt on, I dug into the basket to eat. Taking one of the large strawberry-cinnamon rolls out, I sat on the blanket and chomped into the soft pastry.

Baine stood across from me, arms folded, staring off into the distance.

He was going to make this difficult.

Wiping the sugary glaze off my lips, I opened the water skin and guzzled the fresh liquid, swirling it around my mouth to remove any bits of strawberries from my teeth. When I was sated, and sure I was ready to discuss this whole mate business, I walked over to Baine.

"Are we going to talk about this?" I folded my arms, mimicking his stance.

Instead of answering, he gazed at me, intense, and took a slow step closer. With each step, the intensity of his gaze deepened until I got so flustered, I thought I would trip over my own feet. Taking me by the waist, he dragged me into his embrace and kissed me.

Long, tender, and full of everything joyous in the world. With his powerful hands grasping me, tantalizing me with thoughts I shouldn't have about anyone, I knew in that moment, there would be no one else, *ever*.

Our kisses shifted from soft and gentle to urging. A breeze blew around us, lifting our hair and tickling our necks. His mouth moved from mine, trailing across my cheek to my ear to my neck, and I knew that if I didn't ask my questions now, I'd be lost to the desire burning through my core.

With great difficulty I pulled away, causing Baine to glare at me, his hooded gaze making me question my decision to stop. No matter how delicious he tasted on my lips, I needed answers.

"You called me your mate," I reminded him, watching his reaction carefully. "I don't know about the fae, but I know a lot of the other races mate for life."

He touched his forehead to mine. "We do. It is no easy thing."

With a deep sigh, he wrapped me in a hug, holding me close. "I cannot change how I feel, but I won't force you into any commitment."

Dragging a hand up my back, he gently touched my neck and tilted it back so we could look at one another. "How do you feel about me?"

"The moment you went through that portal, I thought I'd lost you. I never want to lose you again. Stay with me, today, tomorrow, and every day after."

His lip curled into a grin and his lavender gaze sent a shiver through my body. "I promise to never leave you again. You are mine, *forever*."

And with those four words, he swept me off the ground and never put me back down.

The End

Thank you for reading!

Make sure to sign up for my newsletter where

you can get sneak peeks, prizes, and much more.
http://eepurl.com/ghabvr

To continue the adventure grab the next story in *The Shifting Fae series: The Starlit City*

A human sorceress. A dark fae mage. A deadly war that will seal their fates forever.

Kelia is one of the Magi Council's top sorceress and they've sent her to the underground City of Stars to retrieve a prodigal child from the dark fae. The child is the key to the spell that will close the Rift in the Never for good.

To make it to the city, Kelia will need the aid of a dangerous mercenary named Callum whose last twenty years were spent in a magi prison. The Queen demanded his release in exchange for the child, and not even the magi understand why. He's shifty, untrustworthy, disgustingly handsome, and Kelia will need more than her arcane tricks to keep Callum focused on the journey ahead.

When they reach the underground city, and straight into war, their darkest fears become real. If they want to survive, they'll need to learn to trust in each other and combine their hearts and spells to stop the deadly siege.

If not, they'll never see the surface again.

ACKNOWLEDGMENTS

I haven't written an acknowledgement page in awhile, but I felt this book needed it. I had a lot of amazing support and help re-writing this series and I truly wanted to thank those all involved.

To my lovely editor and friend Janella who read the original story and this new version, you've been an amazing shoulder to lean on and you never get sick of reading my stuff—no matter how many times I re-write it. Thank you for everything.

Lori . . . my friend and mentor in all cover things. You've been so patient with my questions and we all know a book is nothing without a pretty cover. One day I'll get to your level, but first I need a Wacom tablet :)

To my BETA readers. You all are so important to the process and your suggestions helped re-shaped the story, even when I thought I was done. Kelly, Harley, Julie, and C Lee. There are not enough thank yous in the world.

And lastly to my writing partner, the man who reads and edits my romance books even though he hates the genre, this story would not be where it is today without your epic plotting skills. Not only do you support everything I do, but you make sure my books are the best that they can be. We really are the dynamic duo and I can't wait until you steal these characters like you did with Avikar.

Thank you to my readers, especially those who read this new version. The last few years have been difficult, but YOU keep me going. I hope you enjoy this series as much as I enjoyed creating this world.

About the Author

USA Today Bestselling author Eliza Tilton graduated from Dowling College with a BA in Visual Communications. When she's not arguing with excel at her day job, chasing after four kids, or playing video games, she's writing fast-paced young adult fantasy and paranormal tales. Check out www.elizatilton.com for more of her books or follow her on tiktok @elizatilton where she shares tons of bookish stuff.